Holly

Kitten Friends

Illustrated by Sophy Williams

Stripes

Other titles by Holly Webb

The Snow Bear

The Reindeer Girl

The Winter Wolf

The Storm Leopards

Animal Stories:

Lost in the Snow

Alfie all Alone

Lost in the Storm

Sam the Stolen Puppy

Max the Missing Puppy

Sky the Unwanted Kitten

Timmy in Trouble

Ginger the Stray Kitten

Harry the Homeless Puppy

Buttons the Runaway Puppy

Alone in the Night

Ellie the Homesick Puppy

Jess the Lonely Puppy

Misty the Abandoned Kitten

Oscar's Lonely Christmas

Lucy the Poorly Puppy

Smudge the Stolen Kitten

The Rescued Puppy

The Kitten Nobody Wanted

The Lost Puppy

The Frightened Kitten

The Secret Puppy

The Abandoned Puppy

The Missing Kitten

The Puppy Who was Left Behind

The Kidnapped Kitten

The Scruffy Puppy

The Brave Kitten

The Forgotten Puppy

The Secret Kitten

A Home for Molly

Sammy the Shy Kitten

The Seaside Puppy

My Naughty Little Puppy:

A Home for Rascal

New Tricks for Rascal

Playtime for Rascal

Rascal's Sleepover Fun

Rascal's Seaside Adventure

Rascal's Festive Fun

Rascal the Star

Rascal and the Wedding

Contents

1   Lost in the Snow   7

2   Smudge the Stolen Kitten   129

3   The Kitten Nobody Wanted   255

www.hollywebbanimalstories.com

STRIPES PUBLISHING
An imprint of Little Tiger Press
1 The Coda Centre, 189 Munster Road,
London SW6 6AW

A paperback original
First published in Great Britain in 2016

Text copyright © Holly Webb
Lost in the Snow 2006
Smudge the Stolen Kitten 2011
The Kitten Nobody Wanted 2011
Illustrations copyright © Sophy Williams
Lost in the Snow 2006
Smudge the Stolen Kitten 2011
The Kitten Nobody Wanted 2011
Illustrations copyright © Kate Pankhurst
Author photograph copyright © Nigel Bird

ISBN: 978-1-84715-713-3

A CIP catalogue record for this book is available
from the British Library.

Printed and bound in the UK.

10 9 8 7 6 5 4 3 2 1

Lost in the Snow

For Sammy and Marble, and for the original Rosie

Chapter One

Rosebridge Farm was a beautiful place in the autumn. The leaves on the big oak tree at the corner of the farmyard had turned golden, and every so often a few of them would whirl down to the ground and give the hens a fright. The farm was a lovely old place, and the Moffat family had been dairy farmers there for over a hundred years.

There were stables, and a big barn, and a beautiful old farmhouse that looked cosy and inviting in the autumn sunshine.

But today no one at the farm was noticing how lovely it all was. Mrs Moffat and her son Ben were in the office, looking at the accounts, and worrying. It had been a difficult year, and money was tight. Outside in the yard, Sara, Mrs Moffat's thirteen-year-old daughter, was trying to give the hen house a makeover. "Ow!" she yelped, as she hit herself with the hammer for the fourth time. "Sorry, chicks," she said to the hens, who were scratching and pecking round her feet. "You're just going to have to wait for Ben to come and help me." She put down the hammer and headed off to the farmhouse, but as she passed the stables something made her stop.

What was that funny squeaking noise? Sara peered over the half-door at Gus, their old pony. He gazed back, and snorted, shaking himself all over. Then he nosed down at a pile of straw practically underneath him. His face seemed to be saying that he wasn't complaining, but really, of all the places...

"Rosie! You've had the kittens!" exclaimed Sara excitedly. She leaned so far over the door she nearly fell into the stable. Rosie the farm cat glared at her. "Sorry, sorry! I promise I won't come in and disturb you. I just want to have a quick look."

The kittens were snuggled up next to Rosie in Gus's bed of straw. They were tripping over each other, as they nuzzled gently at their mother, still blind and helpless.

"Oh, they're gorgeous, Rosie! So how many are there? Two black ones, a ginger – oh no, two gingers. I wish you'd hold still, kittens, I'm counting. And a tabby – oh. Oh dear." Sara's delighted voice flattened. The tabby kitten was so tiny – much, much smaller than her brothers and sisters – and she was hardly moving.

"Oh, I do hope you'll be all right!" Sara whispered worriedly, as one of the others climbed over it. But she had a horrible feeling that the tiny thing was just too small to survive…

Even though Sara had lived on the farm all her life, and she knew that this sort of thing just happened sometimes, her eyes filled with tears.

The littlest kitten was so sweet – it had really long fur and looked like a little bundle of fluff! As she watched, it got trodden on again, and opened its mouth in a tiny, almost silent mew of protest. Sara wiped her sleeve across her eyes sadly.

She took one last look at the kittens – at least the other four looked fit and healthy – and dashed off to tell her mum and Ben.

"Rosie's had her kittens!" she called, as she opened the kitchen door.

Mrs Moffat popped her head round the door of the office. "Oh lovely! How many are there?"

"Five, but—"

"Five more mouths to feed," a gloomy voice sighed. Ben was at agricultural college, training in farm management. He loved Rosebridge Farm, all the Moffats did, but he hated it that things weren't going well. The farm was hardly making enough money to live on at the moment, and Ben was counting every penny.

"Oh, they're only tiny mouths, Ben! We can feed five little kittens!" laughed his mother.

"I think it might only be four soon," said Sara. "The little tabby one – it's so small. I'm not sure it'll make it."

"Oh dear," said Mrs Moffat, jumping up and coming out to the kitchen. "Let's take a look, Sara, where are they?"

Sara led her mum and Ben out to see the new family, hoping that her mum would say she was making a fuss about nothing. But Mrs Moffat looked at the littlest kitten sadly. "I think you might be right, Sara. It's too little. What a pity."

"Please don't call her an it, Mum, I'm sure she's a little girl kitten."

"I know what you mean, she's so pretty and delicate, with those lovely brown and black markings." Mrs Moffat sighed.

"Isn't there anything we can do?" Sara asked, tears filling her eyes again.

"Well, I suppose we could try her with some of that special kitten milk out of an eye-dropper," her mum said doubtfully. "That's if Rosie will let us. But Sara, listen, you mustn't let yourself get too attached to her. I'm really sorry, but her chances just aren't good."

Over the next couple of weeks, Sara wondered if Rosie had heard them saying that the tabby kitten wasn't likely to survive. Rosie was a stubborn old cat, and she seemed determined to prove everyone wrong. She always made sure that the tabby kitten got an extra turn suckling, and by the time the kittens were three weeks old and starting to explore the stable, the littlest kitten was still little, but she was catching up. Rosie was very protective of them, but she did let Sara and her mum in to feed the tabby, and cuddle them all every so often. The littlest kitten fought for more than her fair share of cuddles, and would lie in Sara's arms, purring a purr that seemed far too loud for such a tiny creature.

It wasn't long before the bigger kittens got bored with exploring the stable and playing tag round Gus's hooves, and started trying to escape outside.

One morning the two ginger boy kittens hid behind the stable door. As soon as Sara opened it, they shot out into the farmyard. They seemed a bit surprised by how much world there was out there, but they certainly weren't going back in. Rosie seemed to realize that she couldn't keep them all shut up any longer, so she shooed the other kittens out too. But the tabby cried, and hid behind Rosie – outside was just too big and scary.

Rosie nudged the little kitten to the door, where she mewed miserably, her tiny paws scrabbling as she fought to get back into the safety of the cosy stable.

"Rosie, don't be such a bully!" said Sara, scooping up the trembling kitten. "Poor little ball of fluff, she's scared."

The kitten snuggled into Sara's fleece – this was a much better place to be. And she'd heard that word "fluff" again. Everyone seemed to say it when they saw her. *Perhaps Fluff is my name?* she thought happily.

Sara, Ben and Mrs Moffat had decided not to give any of the kittens names, as they knew that they wouldn't be at the farm for very long. As soon as the kittens were eight weeks old, they'd be old enough to leave Rosie, and find new homes.

But it was hard not to call the little one Fluff. Sara gave in first, and Ben and her mum told her off about it.

"I told you not to get attached to any of them!" her mum scolded. "If you give her a name you'll want her to stay, and you know we can't afford it."

"Eating us out of house and home as it is," muttered Ben, stroking the little kitten under the chin, and trying not to grin as her massive purr rumbled round the stable.

"But she just is a Fluff!" cried Sara, grinning. "Look at her, she's the world's fluffiest kitten!"

It was true. And Fluff had beautiful markings too; a fluffy brown and black tabby coat, huge white paws, and a white shirt-front. She'd inherited Rosie's dark brown eyes, and although she had a huge purr, her mew was still the same tiny little noise that had broken Sara's heart the day she'd been born.

It seemed no time at all before the kittens were eight weeks old. Fluff was still small compared to the others, and she looked even smaller because she seemed to be all fluff, whereas her brothers and sisters had short silky-smooth coats. Sara watched them as they played in the yard. The two black girl kittens were exploring an old bucket, while the two ginger boys played tug of war with a piece of string. As usual, Fluff was sat on her own watching her brothers and sisters, too timid to join in. Sara sighed ... she couldn't help feeling sorry for the little kitten, she always seemed to be left out of their fun and games.

Mrs Moffat and Ben appeared at the back door with steaming mugs of tea. "I know you'd like to keep them all, Sara, but I think the kittens are big enough to leave Rosie now," said Mrs Moffat, as she watched them playing.

"I'll put a sign up on the gate, saying they're free to good homes. I can put up the signs for Christmas wreaths at the same time – making those always brings in extra money at this time of year. And we need every penny," she smiled.

Sara and Ben made faces. The farm was on the outskirts of Fairford, and lots of people came to buy holly wreaths and mistletoe at Christmas. The wreaths made a lot of money, but it meant spending December with prickled fingers.

"It's a pity," Ben said, watching Fluff half-heartedly chase a piece of string. "I shouldn't think anyone will want the little fluffy one – she's so skinny, she looks half-starved."

"How can you be so cruel, she's gorgeous!" Sara protested. But secretly, she couldn't help hoping Ben was right. Fluff was her favourite and she couldn't imagine her out there in the big wide world beyond the farm.

Chapter Two

Fluff and the other kittens knew that they would all be leaving to go to new homes soon. Whenever there were visitors they had to be on their best behaviour in the hope that someone might want to take them home. It had been the same with Rosie's last litter of kittens.

Fluff wasn't sure about it all. She

loved Rosebridge Farm. But then a home of her own did sound wonderful. Fluff's brothers and sisters were very excited, and kept trying to sneak out when the gates were open.

Every time there was a customer for the lovely Christmas wreaths, Mrs Moffat would point out the kittens, frisking prettily in the yard. It wasn't long before the two black girl kittens were snapped up by a lady who fell in love with them as they wove themselves round her legs.

It looked so easy, Fluff thought, and the next day she waited for a friendly-looking customer and tried it for herself. But she tripped the man up, and he stomped off with wet and muddy trousers.

The ginger kittens found owners a few days later, and Fluff watched them being carried away in a beautiful basket. She felt very alone. Rosie was still there, and Gus, and the hens, but it wasn't the same without her brothers and sisters. Even though they'd laughed at her, Fluff missed them. She took to sitting on top of Gus's half-door, and moping.

Rosie tried to persuade her back down, but Fluff preferred to stay where she was. Rosie gave up eventually, but when they curled up in the hay to sleep that night, she was extra-affectionate to Fluff, nuzzling her comfortingly. The big tabby cat wrapped her tail round her last little kitten, and purred as she drifted off to sleep.

But Fluff lay awake, fretting. She knew that her mother was disappointed to have such a skinny, nervous kitten. What was going to happen to her? Mrs Moffat kept looking at her worriedly, and Fluff couldn't help thinking, *What happens to kittens that nobody wants?*

A few days later, Fluff was perched up on Gus's door when a car drew up outside the farmyard. Fluff had given up trying to look lovable, as no one seemed to be interested in taking her home, so she stayed put and just watched.

A lady and her daughter had come to buy a holly wreath. The girl, who was about seven, ran round excitedly, desperate to explore. She poked her head into the hen house, and climbed the fence to look at the cows. Then she began exploring the yard. Her mum kept calling her back – "Ella! Don't get in the way! Ella! Don't get your shoes muddy!" – but Ella wasn't listening.

Then she saw Fluff.

"Oh, what a pretty kitten! Please can I stroke you? Puss?"

A pretty kitten? Does she mean me? Fluff was so surprised that she turned round to see if there was another kitten behind her, forgetting how carefully she was balanced on top of the door… She mewed frantically and clawed her way back up again.

"I'm sorry, I didn't mean to scare you, poor little bundle of fluff…"

Fluff looked at Ella in amazement. This girl knew her name! She reached out to the girl's hand and butted against it with her head, purring delightedly.

"Oh, aren't you sweet? Can I pick you up?" Ella asked, gently.

She certainly could! Fluff snuggled into her neck and licked her chin, making Ella giggle. She tickled Fluff's bright white shirt-front. "The sign outside said they needed homes for kittens. Maybe I could take you home? Mum and Dad promised I could have a pet soon, and you would be perfect."

Fluff purred blissfully. Someone wanted to take her home! Someone who was very, very good at stroking.

Please take me home! she mewed.

Ella carried Fluff back over to her mother, who was paying Mrs Moffat for the wreath.

"Oh, your little girl's found Fluff," said Mrs Moffat hopefully. "We're looking for a home for her, I don't suppose you—"

"Ella! Put that grubby little kitten down!" said Ella's mother in horror.

Grubby? Fluff laid her ears back. She wasn't grubby, was she? She opened her eyes wide at Ella's mother, and tried to look clean.

"Mum, she's not grubby, she's beautiful! Can't we take her home, please? She needs a home, and you did say I could have a pet soon."

"Yes, I know, but not a cat, Ella! A goldfish, maybe. Something nice and clean. And quiet."

"But I don't want a fish! I don't like fish, they're boring. You know I love cats, and Fluff's perfect. Please? I'll look after her."

"No, Ella, I'm sorry, but we don't want a cat in the house. Now come on, we've got Christmas shopping to do."

"Mum, please!" Ella begged.

"No! Now put her down."

Ella's eyes filled with tears, but she put Fluff down gently, kissing the top of her head.

"I'm sorry, Fluff. I'd love to take you home, I think you're beautiful." Ella gave the little tabby one last stroke.

Fluff couldn't believe it. She watched Ella leave, confused, and mewing frantically. "Come back! Come back!" Someone had wanted her, wanted to give her a home. And now they were gone!

Chapter Three

That evening, Ella's mum was starting to wish that she'd never taken Ella to Rosebridge Farm. Ella had spent the rest of the day talking non-stop about Fluff, and when her dad arrived home from work, she didn't even give him the chance to take off his coat.

"Dad, you have to talk to Mum! You did say I could have a pet, didn't you?

You promised! I've found the best pet ever, and Mum says I can't have her, and you have to help me persuade her!"

Ella's dad sighed. He had a feeling that this was one of those situations where he was going to get into trouble whatever he said. "Er, have you? That's nice," he murmured cautiously.

"No, it isn't! Because Mum says I can't have her, you have to talk to her!"

Ella grabbed his arm and dragged him into the kitchen.

Ella's mum was reading a magazine. She had been ignoring Ella entirely for the last hour, because however many times she explained that they couldn't have a cat, it didn't seem to be sinking in. She gave her husband a Look, which meant, "Don't you dare!"

Ella's dad plonked himself down at the table, and sighed. "Ella, I'm sorry, but I have no idea what you're talking about. Come and sit down and tell me again."

Ella huffed irritably, and grabbed the nearest chair. "You said I could have a pet. I've found the pet I want. So can I have her, please?" she said, in a pleading voice.

Ella's dad took a deep breath. "Ella, you know there's more to it than that. Mum and I did say you could have a pet, but it's got to be the right sort of pet."

"But this is the right sort of pet! She's beautiful!"

"Er, what is she exactly?"

"A cat, of course! The prettiest kitten ever, Dad! She's got gorgeous big eyes, and great fat paws, and the fluffiest fur you've ever seen. And she's so tiny, and she really needs a home. She's called Fluff. So can we go back to the farm and get her? Please?"

Ella's dad shook his head. "Ella, we said you could have a hamster! Maybe! If you were very good! Not a cat. We don't want a cat!"

Ella looked shocked. She'd been pinning all her hopes on her dad saying yes. "But why not?" she asked in a small voice. "She's such a sweet cat, Dad. You'd love her. Why don't you just come and see—"

"Ella, Dad said no!" her mum put in tiredly. "And I've already said no. You cannot have that cat, or any cat—"

"I don't want any cat! I want Fluff!" Ella said, her eyes tearing up.

She got up from the table and hurried up to her room. She couldn't believe that her parents had said no. Especially when poor Fluff needed a home so badly. What if no one ever came to take her home?

Chapter Four

The next morning, Fluff was still pining for Ella, in spite of Rosie's efforts to cheer her up.

She slunk out of the stable and batted a piece of paper sack backwards and forwards, occasionally summoning up the energy for a bit of a pounce, but it didn't stop her feeling miserable about Ella.

It wasn't long before a car pulled up in the road outside the farm, and a woman and her son appeared in the yard. Fluff didn't take much notice, until she heard the woman asking about kittens.

Mrs Moffat sounded delighted. "Actually, we've just the one left, but she's a dear little thing. She's there, look, playing with that bit of paper."

Mrs Moffat came over and picked Fluff up, stroking her gently and murmuring nice things. Fluff began to purr, even though she still felt sad. How lovely it would be to have someone to pet her like that all the time! These people couldn't be as nice as Ella, but at least they would give her a home. She rubbed a damp paw quickly round her face, and tried to look clean.

"Isn't she cute?" said the woman, tickling Fluff under her chin. "She'll make you a lovely pet, won't she, Nathan?" she said to the boy.

Nathan didn't look convinced. He just glared at Fluff.

"You see, we want Nathan to have a pet to teach him a sense of responsibility," Nathan's mother said to Mrs Moffat. "He's been in a bit of trouble at school, and one of the teachers came up with the idea. A cat will be perfect."

Nathan spoke for the first time. "I don't want a cat. Cats are boring. Can't I have something cool, like a tarantula or a snake?"

"Don't be silly, Nathan," snapped his mother. "You know we all agreed on a cat."

Mrs Moffat began to look doubtful, and Fluff laid her ears back at the sound of the cross voices. She wasn't sure she liked this family after all.

"You know, I'm not sure… If your son doesn't really want Fluff, you might be better off—"

"Really, she'll be fine with us. Nathan will love her, once he gets used to the idea. Perhaps he could hold her?"

Mrs Moffat looked worriedly at Nathan's scowl, but his mother gave him a Look, and he seemed to remember his manners. "Please can I hold her?" he asked politely.

Still slightly unsure, Mrs Moffat handed him Fluff. Nathan held her as though he wasn't quite sure how to, and patted the top of her head. Too hard – Fluff felt grateful she had nice, thick fur to protect her.

"See, isn't she lovely? You'll be friends in no time." Nathan's mother turned to Mrs Moffat. "Could we take her now? I don't suppose you have a box or something that we could carry her home in?"

As soon as his mother and Mrs Moffat had gone to look for a box, Nathan stopped being quite so nice. He held Fluff out at arm's length and made a disgusted face at her.

"I'm not looking after you," he sneered. "Stupid, ratty little thing." He grabbed the scruff of her neck, and poked her angrily. "I'll be stuck with feeding you and everything. Even a dog would be better." He made a growling noise. "Anyway, I won't have to bother for long. Next door's Alsatian will have you for breakfast."

Fluff looked at the boy with huge round eyes. This was not going to be a home, after all. If only she could just stay here! But Mrs Moffat had said all the kittens must go. She needed a proper home. Somewhere with a friendly, loving person to take care of her. She needed to find Ella!

Fluff's fur stood up on end. She hissed angrily at Nathan, then sank a mouthful of sharp little teeth into the finger that he was prodding her with. He yelped and dropped her. Fluff landed lightly on the floor and took a flying leap on to the farmyard wall. She was going to do what Rosie had always forbidden. She took a last look at her old home, and then she jumped down the other side of the wall. Mrs

Moffat and Nathan's mother came back into the yard just in time to see a fluffy tabby tail whisking over the wall, and Nathan looking shocked and guilty.

"Fluff!" Mrs Moffat cried, running to the gate. She wrenched it open and dashed outside. But there was no little kitten waiting to be called back in, no flash of tabby fur disappearing round the corner. Fluff was gone!

Chapter Five

On the other side of Fairford, Ella was lying on her bedroom floor drawing a picture. It was a picture she'd drawn at least twenty times already. Sometimes Fluff was sitting down, sometimes she was walking along the stable door, but she always looked sad. Sad and lonely, just like Ella was feeling. Ella fetched her best water-colouring pencils, and started to colour in Fluff's lovely tabby fur, using a wet paintbrush to make it look soft and fluffy. How could her mum say Fluff was grubby? She was so beautiful! Ella carefully outlined Fluff's big eyes with black, and added her sparkling white whiskers and eyebrows. Then she got out her gel pens, and added a little silver tear trickling out of the corner of each eye.

"Ella, there you are." Ella hadn't even noticed her dad calling for her. It was Saturday, and he'd been out in the garden trimming the Christmas tree, preparing to bring it indoors. "That's beautiful. Is that Fluff?"

Ella nodded, and sniffed, and then a real tear splashed down on to the paper and made Fluff's fur run. It was ruined. Ella blinked back the tears, and sadly scrunched up the piece of paper. She'd given up arguing with her parents about Fluff, because it wasn't doing any good at all, but she couldn't stop being miserable, and worrying about the little kitten.

"Ella, will you come downstairs a minute? Your mum and I want to talk to you."

Ella sighed, but followed her dad downstairs. She knew what they were going to say. Mum and Dad were going to try to cheer her up again like they had earlier. So far, they'd suggested Christmas shopping, decorating the Christmas tree, and a trip to the pantomime. But even though the pantomime had been a fantastic treat, Ella just couldn't stop thinking about Fluff.

Her parents were sitting at the kitchen table, looking serious. Ella's mum took her hand. "Ella, your dad and I know you've been really sad about not being able to have Fluff. We've talked it over, and although we're still a bit worried about it, we've decided that you can have her after all—"

Ella didn't wait to hear more. She threw herself at her mum, knocking the breath out of her. "You mean it? Thank you, thank you, thank you!"

"Ella, listen. You can only have Fluff on the condition that you look after her properly. She'll need feeding twice a day, and grooming, especially if she's as fluffy as you say she is. You'll have to be very responsible." Dad's voice was serious, and Ella nodded.

"I'll look after her, I promise." Ella was beaming. She would do anything!

"Well, what are we waiting for?" Dad bounced up from the table. "Let's go and get her! Why don't we walk over to the farm? It's only a short walk to the other side of town, and it's a beautiful day."

Ella dashed into the hall and put on her pink sheepskin boots, and fluffy winter jacket. She added a hat with ear flaps, and a huge scarf.

Dad laughed. "You look like an Eskimo! But you're right, it's freezing out there. I wouldn't be surprised if it snowed soon. Now where are my gloves?"

Ella was dancing around with impatience by the time her mum and dad were ready. Dad popped next door to borrow their cat basket, and he laughed at Ella's jittery face. "Well, what were you thinking, that you'd just tuck her inside that scarf of yours?" Ella thought that sounded perfect. Finally they were ready to go, walking through town, weaving their way through the bustling shoppers. It was lovely – with Christmas only four days away, everyone was in a festive mood, and all the shop windows were full of presents, tinsel and sparkling Christmas trees.

Ella held her dad's hand, rushing him along. "She's such a pretty kitten, Dad, you'll love her. I'll look after her really well, I promise. Oh, look, there's the sign for the farm. Come on! I can't wait to see her again!"

Ella ran the last little way, and her mum and dad exchanged smiles. They hadn't been sure about letting Ella have a kitten, but she was so happy, it had to be the right decision.

They opened the farm gate, and Ella dashed off to try and find Fluff, while her parents went to look for Mrs Moffat.

"Fluff! Fluff!" Ella called, but no little kitten came running. There was a beautiful big tabby cat, sitting quietly on the stable door, just where Fluff had been when Ella first saw her. Ella went over to her. "You must be Fluff's mum! You have to be, your eyes are just the same. Where is she, puss? We've come to take her home!"

The tabby cat gave Ella a long look, then jumped down from the door and disappeared round the corner of the yard, walking very fast. It was almost as if Ella had upset her.

Just then Ella's mum and dad came out of the farmhouse with Mrs Moffat. "I'm really sorry," she was explaining. "It's such bad luck − really awful timing."

"Oh no! Has someone else taken Fluff home?" Ella gasped.

"N-no – not exactly," said Mrs Moffat, looking worried. "I'm afraid Fluff is lost. Some people came to see about taking her earlier this morning, and I think the boy frightened her. She jumped over the wall and disappeared. She's never even been out of the gates before! I've been searching all around, and so have Ben and Sara, but we can't find her anywhere. It's odd, she's normally such a friendly little thing, I'd have expected her to come running. We'll keep looking, of course, but—"

Ella's dad could see that Ella was about to burst into tears, and he put his arm round her. "If you find her, could you let us know?" he asked. He scribbled their phone number on a bit of paper, and handed it to Mrs Moffat.

"Couldn't we go and look for her?"
Ella begged, as they left the farm. "We
might find her."

"Ella, she could be a long way away
by now," her mum explained. "Mrs
Moffat's already looked all around here.
I'm afraid we haven't got much chance
of finding her."

"But she's so little! And Mrs Moffat said she's never been outside the farm before." Ella started to cry, and her dad hugged her tight.

"Mrs Moffat's going to keep looking. You never know…"

Ella nodded miserably, and shivered. It was so cold. Poor Fluff was out here lost and all alone. How would such a little kitten ever find her way home?

Chapter Six

The minute Fluff had landed on the other side of the wall, she'd set off as fast as her legs would carry her. She wanted to get as far away as possible from that horrible boy and, without knowing it, she'd run into one of the town's main streets, which was packed with Christmas shoppers. Now, Fluff was cowering behind a rubbish bin, watching shoes, all of which were threatening to step on her. She'd been sitting there for ages. She'd never imagined that outside could be so big. There were so many people, and so many cars roaring past. No wonder Rosie had warned them to stay in the yard! She had no idea what she should do next. How on earth was she going to find Ella? Cautiously, she put a paw out of her hiding place, and then whipped it back quickly as another boot came down and nearly squashed it. She squeezed herself back behind the bin and sat there shivering.

Fluff felt like she'd been under there for hours when she finally dared to come out. She felt safer now that it was dark, and there were fewer people about. She sniffed the air hopefully. Food smells were all around, but she had no idea where they were coming from. Back at the farm she would have been fed by now, and her stomach rumbled loudly. She slunk along the edges of the pavement, hiding in the shadows, until finally the shops gave way to houses and gardens. Then she jumped up on to a wall to give herself a view of the street, and settled down for a little rest, and a think about what to do next.

All at once she missed the cosy stable, and the comforting sound of Gus the pony snorting in his sleep. *Oh, why did I ever leave the farm?* Fluff mewed. Then she shook her whiskers firmly. *Because I'm going to find Ella, that's why,* she told herself.

Suddenly she was jolted out of her thoughts by an angry hissing. She spun round at once, her fur fluffing up. A huge tomcat was towering over her, his ginger tail flailing to and fro, and his whiskers bristling.

Fluff gasped. He seemed to be at least three times as big as she was! She mewed hopefully at him. Perhaps he could show her where to find some food. Ducking her head shyly, she crept along the wall towards him.

But the tomcat was anything but friendly. He made a low growling noise as he inched towards her. Then, in one quick movement, he lifted one of his enormous paws and cuffed Fluff round the head, sending her flying. Dazed, Fluff landed badly on the pavement below. She shot off down the road, looking back just once, to see the massive cat hulking on the wall and staring after her.

Fluff didn't stop running until she was at least three roads away. She sneaked under a gate into a garden, and wriggled herself under a bush, her heart thumping. She was only a kitten, and she had no idea about life outside the farm. How was she to know that the wall belonged to the tomcat? Did everywhere outside belong to somebody else? She tried to snuggle down into the old dead leaves under the bush, but she couldn't relax, and she spent the rest of the night dozing, and then waking in a panic every time she heard a rustle of leaves, or the squawk of a night bird. *I shouldn't have run away*, Fluff thought to herself. *Even that boy couldn't be as bad as this? Could he?*

Only a few streets away, Ella's parents were sitting in their warm kitchen drinking a cup of tea together. Ella's mum frowned. "I really don't know what to do to cheer her up," she sighed. "It's not that she's being sulky, or difficult, or anything like that – she just seems so sad."

Ella's dad nodded. "What's really upset her is that Fluff's out there lost and all alone. Ella's frightened for her."

"And I have a horrible feeling that Mrs Moffat won't be able to find her," worried Ella's mum. "I know I didn't really want Ella to have a cat, but it's so sad that it's turned out like this. It's so cold out there at the moment, and—

Goodness, what was that? Did you hear a noise out in the hall?"

They jumped up from the table and hurried out of the kitchen.

"Ella! What on earth are you doing? You're supposed to be in bed!"

Ella was standing on a pile of books, trying to undo the security chain on the front door. She was wearing her pyjamas tucked into her purple wellies, and her eyes were blotchy from crying.

"I've got to find Fluff!" she said desperately, scrabbling at the chain. "Can we go out and look for her?" The street light was casting strange blue and green shadows through the stained-glass panels in the door, and Ella looked like a little ghost.

"Ella, it's ten o'clock! And it's freezing outside!" Ella's mum started to help her down from her makeshift ladder.

"I know!" Ella wailed. "But Fluff's out there, Mum, all on her own. Please let me go out and look for her!"

"Ella, you can't go out there in the dark," said her dad firmly. "Anyway, someone else might have found Fluff; she could be fine. But I promise I'll take you out looking for her tomorrow. And Mum will ring the farm and see if they've had any more news." He tightened the security chain carefully. "That's only if you go straight back to bed now."

Ella cast one longing look back at the door, and reluctantly sat down on the stairs to take off her wellies. "You promise?"

"Definitely. We'll do our best to find her, just not now."

Ella nodded, and trailed sadly back up the stairs, carrying her books.

Chapter Seven

Fluff woke with a start, to find that it was getting light. She shivered as she remembered why she wasn't curled up in the cosy stable with Rosie. She stretched painfully, stiff with cold, and started on a quick morning wash. It was while she was busy with the delicate job of behind her ears that she realized what the strange feeling in her middle must be. She hadn't had anything to eat since yesterday's breakfast, and she was starving! She needed to find some food very soon. She could smell that there were mice about, but she didn't think she had much chance of catching one. But that bin she'd sheltered under yesterday had had food smells coming from it. She set off out of the garden to find a bin.

It wasn't long before she came to a litter-bin attached to a lamp-post. Fluff sniffed hopefully – it had a definite foody whiff. It took several goes, but after a flying leap, and a lot of scrabbling, Fluff found herself balanced on the edge of the bin, catching her breath. She took a deep sniff – cheese! Sara had occasionally given her a nibble of cheese from her sandwiches, and there was definitely cheese in this bin. There was another odd smell as well, a little like mouse, but Fluff wasn't quite sure what it was.

Fluff leaned over, balancing as carefully as she could. Yes, there it was! Half a cheese sandwich! She reached out a delicate paw and hooked it out triumphantly. She was just about to jump down and drag the sandwich away somewhere quiet when there was a sudden scuffling noise underneath her, and the rubbish moved.

An enormous rat popped up from under a hamburger box, and bared his dirty great teeth at Fluff. Then he snatched the sandwich back, and hissed at her.

Fluff lost her balance and slid off backwards, twisting frantically in the air, but still landing painfully and jarring her paws. She raced off down the road, sure she could still hear the rat's horrible hissing in her ear.

At last, out of breath, and with her paws aching, she scuttled under a parked car to hide. *What am I going to do?* she panicked to herself. *I can't find anywhere safe to sleep, or anything to eat, and I can't find Ella! Maybe I should just go back?* She missed Rosie, and Gus the pony, and everyone at the farm. And right this minute, she really missed the food, and her warm bed in the stable!

The farm was the only home she'd ever known, and all she had to do was go back the way she'd come. Surely that boy would have gone by now. *Maybe they'll be glad to see me back?* she thought. *They might even let me stay!* She set off, retracing her steps, but crossing to the other side of the road and running to avoid the litter-bin and the scary rat. Those first few streets weren't too hard, but when Fluff got back to the garden where she'd slept under a bush, nothing looked familiar. Which way had she come from? Where was the tomcat's wall? Fluff shivered with cold. She looked down the road one way, and then the other. She hadn't a clue – but it was getting so cold and she had to make a decision. She set off again, hoping that she would come across something that she remembered. But a few streets later Fluff found herself trotting past a little row of shops that she was certain she'd never seen before. She paused on the edge of the pavement to try and work out when she'd made her mistake.

Suddenly, there was a loud roaring noise and a car shot past her, skidding through a deep, muddy puddle, and soaking Fluff to the skin in dirty water. She gasped in shock as she felt the cold biting into her. She shuddered, and looked round desperately for a warm place to dry off.

A lady with a big shopping bag was going into one of the shops, and Fluff felt the gust of warmth as the door opened. *Surely they wouldn't mind if I just went in to get warm,* she thought to herself. *I won't stay long.*

The shop was brightly lit, and it looked so inviting that Fluff couldn't resist. She hurried over and followed the lady in, sneaking along behind her shopping bag.

It was so nice to be somewhere warm again! She peeped around the side of the bag, and gulped with delight. There was a bowl of food at the corner of the counter! Fluff didn't stop to think. She darted over to the bowl and started to gobble as fast as she could.

She'd managed a few mouthfuls, when a strange rrrrr-ing noise made the fur on the back of her neck lift up. She froze in panic, her heart thumping. There wasn't a dog on the farm, and Fluff had never met one before, but some deep cat instinct stirred inside her.

The rrrrr-ing changed to a deep woof, and suddenly an enormous creature flung itself at Fluff, barking madly and baring its teeth.

The lady with the bag and the shop-owner looked down in amazement. "What's the matter with you, Fergus, you daft dog? Oh my goodness! Where did that scrawny little thing come from? And it's stealing your dinner! Shoo, you nasty stray. Go on, Fergus, chase it out, it's probably full of fleas!" The man flung the door open and Fergus (who was only a dachshund, but thought he was at least a Great Dane) chased Fluff out on to the pavement, his teeth only inches from her tail.

When Fluff dared to look back, she was surprised to see that the dog wasn't actually much bigger than she was. It wasn't fair! Why shouldn't she have had some of that nice food too? There had been plenty for them both. She skidded to a stop and spat angrily at Fergus. She was sick of running away. She stood nose to nose with the little dog and snarled, her tail twitching. Then as he started to bark again, she shot out a paw and raked her tiny claws down his muzzle.

Fergus howled with shock. The little cat was supposed to run off shaking like a jelly, not fight back! He wailed again, and his owner, who'd been watching from the door, flung a newspaper at Fluff, yelling, "Get out of here, you horrible stray!"

Fluff dodged the newspaper, but the man's words hit her. She'd been too busy running the first time he'd called her a stray, but now it struck home. She slunk off into the shadows, feeling more alone than ever. She was a stray!

She knew all about strays. No one wanted them, and Rosie chased them away if they came to the farm. If Fluff was a stray cat now, maybe she wouldn't be welcome at the farm after all...

Chapter Eight

Fluff padded sadly along the pavement. She was a little less hungry after the food she'd stolen from Fergus's bowl, but she was still frozen. It was already getting dark again, and it seemed even colder than the night before. Fluff decided to look for somewhere to hide for the night, and think about what to do in the morning.

She trotted down a dark alleyway, with a row of bins down one side.

The alley was full of good smells, but about halfway down Fluff noticed another smell that somehow wasn't so good. In fact, it was almost a scary smell. She took a deep sniff, trying to work out what it was. It was a little bit like the smell of Fergus, but not quite. Stronger and – dirtier, somehow… She lifted her head, sensing that someone was watching her, and gulped.

A huge fox was peering at her round the nearest rubbish bin, his tongue lolling, and a hungry gleam in his eye. He had Fluff cornered, and they both knew it.

Fluff froze in panic for a second. He was enormous!

Then she shot backwards, and
squeezed herself into a tiny space
between two bins, where the fox
wouldn't be able to get in. Did foxes eat

kittens? Fluff wasn't sure, but this one was looking at her as though she might make a tasty snack. He stuck his nose into Fluff's hidey-hole, eyeing her all the while. Then he scrabbled a paw in, and then his shoulder, and then he barged one of the bins out of the way, knocking it over. He grinned at Fluff, showing his enormous teeth.

Fluff was trapped, but she wasn't giving up. She'd seen off Fergus, hadn't she? She fluffed up her fur and hissed defiantly, as much to make herself feel brave as anything else. The fox crept closer, and Fluff batted at it angrily with one tiny paw. It was like hitting a rock. This was no Fergus, about to turn tail. But there was nothing else she could do...

Fluff hissed and spat as well as she knew how, and amazingly, after a few seconds the fox stopped. He seemed confused. He put his head on one side, and watched her, a puzzled look in his eyes. Then, slowly, he started to make a strange barking noise, and crouched down with his long muzzle resting on his paws.

Fluff gazed at him, confused and scared. What was he doing? It sounded almost like − was he laughing at her? She edged as far back as she could into the shelter of the bins, not sure what to do next. The fox watched, his nose still on his paws, and gave an encouraging yap. Then he wriggled backwards on his haunches, giving her a clear space to escape.

Fluff watched, puzzled. Was he not
going to eat her after all? He looked
almost friendly. Suddenly the fox
sprang up, and Fluff squashed herself
backwards against the wall, trembling.
But instead of launching himself at the
bin, the fox turned tail and disappeared
off down the alley. Fluff waited a
moment, then poked her nose gingerly
out of her hiding place, and peered

round. The fox was coming back, his white-tipped tail waving jauntily, and in his mouth was a piece of ham. It was chewed and smelly, but it looked delicious. Fluff's whiskers twitched with longing.

The fox laid the ham down in front of Fluff, and retreated.

Was this a trap? Was he going to pounce as soon as she was out of her shelter? Fluff eyed the ham, and tried to measure the distances. But her tummy was telling her to forget being careful and go for the food! She darted swiftly out, grabbed the ham and ran back to the bins. The fox just watched, making that odd barking noise again. He hadn't even tried to catch her. Maybe he was friendly? Fluff shivered.

This was the first friendly creature she'd met since she left the farm. It seemed strange that it should be a huge, scary fox.

The fox disappeared again, and Fluff watched eagerly this time. Was he going to get more food? The fox trotted back, holding something in his mouth carefully. He set it down gently, and pushed it towards her – a half-full tin of tuna! This time Fluff didn't hesitate. The smell of the fish was too good to resist. The fox watched admiringly as Fluff wolfed it down, licking the edges of the tin to catch the last morsels.

As Fluff licked the delicious juice from her whiskers, a huge yawn overtook her, and she stretched. Now that she wasn't so hungry, she realized how tired she was. But she still had nowhere to sleep.

The fox watched her thoughtfully, head on one side. Then he gave an encouraging yap, and jerked his head. Fluff looked back cautiously. He seemed to want her to follow him. She wasn't sure whether it was safe, but she was just so tired. Perhaps the fox was going to show her somewhere she could rest. She set off after the fox, too sleepy to worry any more. He led her off down the alley, looking back every so often to nod and twitch his ears at her.

They scrabbled under a fence – it was much easier for Fluff than it was for the fox – and into an overgrown garden. The fox threaded his way through the brambles, and then stood back proudly. He'd brought her to his den! It was a comfy hole under a garden shed, and it smelled horribly of fox. But Fluff was in no position to be choosy. The fox gave her a gentle nudge with his long nose, and she crept inside, snuggling down into an old sack. The fox looked in after her, as if to check she was all right, and then trotted off. Fluff guessed he was going to find his own food.

Despite the smell, Fluff slept until it was light. Then she woke and stretched sleepily, confused for a moment about where she was. Of course! The fox's hole! And it looked as though he'd left her a snack. Lying by her nose was a bit of old kipper. Fluff nibbled it gratefully, still wondering why the fox had turned out to be so friendly. She stuck her nose out from under the shed and sniffed the fresh morning air. It was a nice change after the foxy whiff of the den. After a good sleep, and something to eat, Fluff was feeling much better. She was sure she would find Ella today. She wished the fox had come back so she could say goodbye, but there was no sign of him.

But if I don't find Ella, she thought, *I'll have no trouble finding my way back to see the fox again. I'll just follow the smell!*

Chapter Nine

"So, no news then?" Ella's mum said into the phone. Ella sat on the kitchen worktop beside her, desperately trying to hear what Mrs Moffat was saying. "No, it's awful, isn't it? Ella and her dad went out yesterday looking for Fluff, all around the town. They were out for hours, but they didn't even find anyone who'd spotted her. Well, thanks for trying, and do let us know if you hear anything." She put the phone down. "They haven't seen her, I'm afraid. Don't look so sad, Ella, someone else might have found her! She could be having a lovely breakfast right this minute. Which reminds me – eat some of yours."

"I'm not hungry," Ella said sadly, as she went back to her breakfast and started pushing her Rice Krispies round the bowl. "Can we go out and put up the posters I made of Fluff?"

"Yes. *When* you've eaten your breakfast," her mother added, as Ella leaped down from the worktop.

Ella sat down and started to shovel in her cereal as fast as she could.

"And always assuming you haven't

choked to death on a Rice Krispie," her mother sighed.

They walked over towards the farm to start with, and then came back along the main street. It was another freezing cold day, and even Ella was starting to flag after an hour of sticking posters of Fluff on to every lamp-post they could find. They all said the same thing:

Several people stopped to look and say how cute the little kitten was, but no one had seen her. When they got to the playground, a few streets from their house, Ella's mum persuaded her to call it a day. "Lots of people will see all those posters. We need to get back home before we freeze. Come on, we'll go home and have some hot chocolate to warm us up. And then you promised to help me sort out all that old junk in the garage, remember?"

Ella nodded sadly. She'd really hoped that they would spot Fluff, but there'd been no sign of her. Ella tucked the roll of Sellotape back into her pocket, and put her gloves on. Her hands were going numb, and she shivered. Poor little Fluff. Mum and Dad kept saying that someone had probably found her by now, but what if she was still out in the cold?

Fluff was outside, and she was frozen. She'd set out from the fox's den that morning feeling very confident, but an hour later, she was running out of energy. She plodded on, her paws starting to feel tired again, and then, at the end of the road, she heard a noise that gave her some hope. She broke into a run, and rounded the corner, following the laughter and yells to a playground. A group of children, all wearing winter coats and scarves, were rushing about madly to keep warm.

Fluff crouched down by the gate, searching the faces for Ella, but there was no sign of her. As she watched, still more children arrived. It seemed that every child in the neighbourhood was coming and going from the playground. So surely Ella would come there too? She settled herself under one of the benches round the edge of the playground, and prepared to keep watch. Some of the children tried to coax her out, but she wouldn't come. One little girl reached under to pat her, but her mother grabbed her, and told her off. "Leave it, Lucy, it's a stray. Look how dirty and matted its fur is. Don't encourage it!"

Several times she got up, ready to rush over to some dark-haired girl muffled up in a coat and hat, and then realized at the last minute that it wasn't Ella. But it wasn't until it began to get dark, and the parents sitting around waiting for their children started to call to them to go home, that Fluff was forced to give up. She felt sure she'd find Ella here – she'd never seen so many children before. She left the playground, following the last of the children, and wandered down the road, trying to think what to do. She didn't know that there was a poster with her picture pinned to every lamp-post.

She was hungry again, and thirsty, so she slipped under a garden gate, and started to look around. The third garden she came to had a birdbath. Fluff leaped up on to the edge and dipped her tongue in. The water was freezing – really freezing, for the edges of the birdbath were icing over. Fluff shivered as she felt the icy water settling in her tummy, and then jumped as something cold landed on her nose. Snow! Fluff had never seen it before, but Rosie had told her about it. She leaped down on to the grass, and couldn't resist jumping and batting at the thick white flakes for a while, but the snow was falling fast, and soon her paws were soaked.

Fluff looked uncertainly towards the house. The windows were brightly lit, and she watched as two children hung up tinsel round the pictures on the walls. There was a plump black cat with them, perched comfortably on the back of the sofa. Fluff could almost hear it purring. She jumped up on to the window sill, which was already coated with a layer of snow, and pressed herself against the glass, desperate to be inside the warm room. The little boy went out, and came back with a sandwich, which he shared with the black cat! Fluff could hardly bear to watch, and she mewed piteously, hoping he would notice her, and let her have some too. But no one heard her. Then the children started a game, wafting the tinsel around for the cat to chase, but all it did was yawn, and put out a paw occasionally.

"I'll chase it," Fluff mewed. "I'll chase it for you properly!" But still they took no notice, and then their mother came in, and drew the curtains, to shut out the dark and cold. No one saw the little brown cat, huddled on the window sill, crying to be let in.

Fluff jumped down, and set off again. She needed to find shelter, out of the snow. In the short time she'd spent on the window sill, those few flakes of snow had thickened to a storm, and the snow already covered her paws as she plodded wearily through it. *I'll find a shed to hide under until this stops*, she decided. But none of the sheds had space to wriggle underneath them like her fox friend's den. She tried hiding behind some bins down the side of a house, but the wind whistled straight through, and it was almost colder than out in the open.

She ducked underneath another fence, and tracked across the next garden. The house was brightly lit, and the lamplight shining through the curtains cast pretty shadows through the blue and green stained glass in the door. *There's probably another fat black cat in there,* Fluff thought sadly. *Probably having its tea.* There were cardboard boxes by the garage, all piled up. One was full of old newspapers, and Fluff looked at it thoughtfully. It wasn't a great place to shelter, but there wasn't much snow on it, and the newspapers did look so comfortable... Perhaps she could just have a little rest?

She clambered in, her legs feeling awkward and clumsy with the cold, and curled up, a tiny ball of damp fur. She hadn't meant to go to sleep, but she was so tired. The snow kept falling, and it wasn't long before even the tips of Fluff's ears were covered. But by then, Fluff had fallen into a deep, cold sleep...

Chapter Ten

Ella had been watching from the window for her dad for nearly an hour by the time he came home.

"Sorry I'm late, sweetheart, there was loads to finish up before the Christmas holiday," he explained as he hugged her.

"Did you see her, Dad? While you were driving home, did you see Fluff?"

"No, Ella, I'm sorry. You didn't have any luck when you went out looking with Mum today, then?"

"No." Ella shook her head sadly. "We went all round, as far as the playground, but we didn't see her. We put Lost posters up everywhere, too, with pictures I drew of Fluff on them."

"Well, we'll go out and look again tomorrow. It's Christmas Eve, and I'll be home all day. Good thing too, the snow's getting quite deep out there."

Ella's mum called from the kitchen, "Is that you, Dave? Don't take your shoes off yet!"

Ella's dad sighed. "What is it? Can't it wait until tomorrow, it's freezing out there! Can't I have a cup of tea and a sit-down?" he called.

"No, because then I'll never get you out again! Ella and I sorted out all that recycling in the garage this afternoon; it took us ages. And now it's outside the garage getting snowed on! Can you put it in the car for me, so we're ready next time we go past the recycling bins?"

"OK, OK," Ella's dad grumbled. He wound his scarf back round his neck, and stepped out into the cold. He hurried over to the pile of boxes, leaving deep footprints in the snow. "They're full of snow already," he called back to Ella, who was peering round the door. "And heavy – ugh!" He picked up one of the boxes and struggled down the path to the car, balancing it on one knee while he unlocked the boot. It took a few trips, but at last he headed back to the house, looking forward to a nice hot cup of tea.

Ella sat at the kitchen table, watching him drink it and looking hopeful. "Ella, it's no good you giving me that look. I'm not taking you out to search for Fluff again now. It's dark!"

"But Dad, you said the snow's getting deep! What if poor Fluff's buried in it?"

Her dad sighed. "Ella. I'm sorry, but if that's the case, then we wouldn't be able to find her, would we? I'm sure someone else will have found her by now. You've put the posters up, so maybe whoever found her will get in touch." He knew that actually it wasn't very likely, but he was desperate to cheer her up. "You know what? I've just remembered that I've got a surprise for you in the car! Come and see!"

"What's the surprise, Dad?" Ella asked as they trekked down the path, trying hard to sound excited. But he only smiled and wouldn't tell her. "Look on the back seat."

As she opened the car door and peered into the back seat, she heard an odd rustling sound from the boot. "Dad? Does my surprise make a noise?"

"What, love?" Ella's dad was stamping his feet to keep warm.

"There was a funny noise from the boot. Is it the surprise?"

"There's nothing in the boot except those boxes of newspapers and things that you and your mum sorted out. It was probably just some snow falling off the roof, or something."

"I'm sure it came from the boot," Ella said doubtfully. She climbed in and peered over the back seat but the parcel shelf was fixed in the way. The rustling sound came again, and Ella jumped, bumping her head on the car roof. "Ow! Dad, I heard it again! There is something in the boot, honestly." Ella wriggled out backwards, feeling a bit nervous. "There's something moving about! Have you got a torch?"

"Well, there's a torch in the glove compartment, but really, Ella, there's nothing there!" He reached into the front of the car and scrabbled around for the torch. "There you go."

Back in the boot, Fluff was stirring. Ella's dad had had the heater on while he was driving home from work, and the car was still quite warm. Warmer than Fluff had been all day. She stretched blissfully in her sleep, and the melting snow slid off her, just as Ella opened the boot and shone the torch inside.

"Wh—! Fluff! Oh, Dad, look, Fluff's in the box! That's the surprise; you've found Fluff! But you told me you hadn't seen her!"

"What? I haven't! My surprise was a big box of chocolates!" Her dad looked confused. "Are you sure?" He peered into the boot. "Well, that's definitely a kitten... How on earth did she get there? You're sure that's Fluff?"

"I'm sure! Oh, Dad, she came to find us, and she went to sleep in the box!" Gently, Ella reached in and lifted the snoozing kitten out. "Oh, she's all wet and freezing! We have to get her dry."

Ella's dad shook his head. "I can't believe she came looking for you. Come on, let's get her inside in the warm."

They rushed back to the house, and into the kitchen. Ella's mum was cooking the dinner, and didn't look round. "So what was the surprise?

Chocolates, perhaps? I could just do with a chocolate."

"Oh! We left them in the car!" Ella giggled, sounding happy for the first time in days. "Sorry, Mum!"

"Mmm, and I've got a complaint, Jen. You said you'd sorted through all that recycling," said Ella's dad, grinning. "Those bins are for bottles and paper only, you know. No kittens allowed."

"What?" Ella's mum spun round and saw Fluff cuddled in Ella's arms. "Oh! I don't believe it! Is that really Fluff? Where was she?"

"In amongst those newspapers, in the boot of the car!"

Fluff was staring blearily around, wondering if she was still dreaming.

But the soft towel that the girl was rubbing her with seemed to be real, and the girl really was Ella! She managed a small purr as the warmth started to seep into her bones.

"We haven't any cat food," said Ella's mum worriedly, opening the kitchen cupboard. "Do you think she'd like tuna?" she said, holding out a tin to Ella. Fluff recognized it at once, and stood up shakily on Ella's lap, mewing hopefully.

"Mmm, well, I'd better find the tin-opener." Ella's mum shook her head in amazement. "I just can't believe we found her!"

"She found us, Mum! It's like a Christmas wish come true." Ella smiled to herself, stroking Fluff's ears. *And we're Fluff's Christmas present*, she thought. *Fluff's got a home for Christmas.*

"We should call the farm and let them know," Ella's dad said, as he searched for an old bowl to put Fluff's tuna in.

"But Dad, what if they want her back?" Ella gasped in horror, and hugged Fluff tightly, making her squeak. "Sorry, Fluff!"

"Don't worry, Ella. I'm sure they'll be delighted for you to keep her. They know how much you wanted Fluff and that you'll take good care of her." Her mum crouched down next to her and tickled Fluff under the chin. "You're right, she's not grubby, she's gorgeous!" She grinned at Ella, remembering the first time she'd seen Fluff. "We just don't want everyone at the farm to worry any more, that's all. Mrs Moffat wanted a good home for Fluff, and now she's got one."

Ella nodded, relieved. "And you'd better remind Mrs Moffat to tell Fluff's mum she's safe. She was really worried." She saw her mum and dad exchange an amused look over her head, but she didn't care. Fluff was home, and nothing else mattered. And Fluff, tucking into the big bowl of tuna, thought so too.

Smudge the Stolen Kitten

For Robin

Chapter One

There was the sound of a whistle blowing. "Ben Williams and Rob Ford! Get down from there right now!"

Olivia looked up and groaned. Mrs Mackintosh sounded as if she'd yelled right in Olivia's ear, even though she was on the other side of the playground.

"What have Ben and Rob done now?" her friend Lucie asked.

"Something awful, as usual," Olivia muttered, as they ran across the playground to see what was going on. Her big brother Ben was always in trouble at school – which wasn't fair, because all the teachers either thought that meant Olivia was naughty too, or that she ought to have stopped him. As if he'd listen to *her*! And his friend Rob was even worse.

"You're very lucky you haven't broken your necks!" the girls heard Mrs Mackintosh saying crossly. "What a stupid thing to do!"

"It isn't in the playground rules that we can't tightrope walk along the top of the fence, Mrs Mackintosh," Ben said innocently, pointing to the poster on the side of the wall.

"That's because before you, Ben, no one had even thought of it!" the head teacher snapped. "We need to add an extra rule at the bottom of that list saying that whatever idiotic thing you two think of next isn't allowed! You can miss the rest of play. Go inside and tell Mrs Beale that you're to help set out the chairs for assembly this afternoon!"

Ben winked at Olivia as he and Rob went past on their way to the hall. He didn't look as though he minded being told off at all.

Olivia sighed and Lucie gave her a sympathetic smile. "It's probably better than having a brother who's totally perfect – then everyone would ask you why you couldn't be more like him."

"I suppose," Olivia sighed, kicking at a pile of leaves. "But I can't wait till he goes to secondary school next year."

"Mrs Beale told me about what happened at lunchtime, by the way." Mum eyed Ben sternly. She worked as a part-time teaching assistant at Olivia and Ben's school.

Ben waved a forkful of spaghetti at her, looking hurt. "It's so unfair! No one had ever said we couldn't walk along the fence."

"Sometimes I think we should just send you and Rob to join the circus." Dad was trying to look cross, but Olivia could see that he was smiling.

"Excellent! No more school!" Ben grinned.

"It wasn't at all clever, Ben." Mum frowned. "I'm tempted not to tell you the special news I've got."

Olivia looked up from her pasta. "What is it? Don't be mean, Mum!"

Her mum stared up at the ceiling smiling, while Olivia and Ben begged her to tell.

"All right, all right! You remember a while ago we had a leaflet through the door about the Cat Rescue Centre?"

Olivia nodded eagerly. "With photos of all the cats they'd found new homes for! They were gorgeous. I wish we could have one. It said they were always looking for good homes for unwanted cats."

Mum smiled. "I know, Olivia – you went on about it for days. Well, Dad and I have been talking, and we decided that maybe you're both old enough to have a pet."

"Really?" Olivia gasped. "We're going to get a cat?"

"I'd rather have a dog, Mum," Ben put in. "Dogs are more fun."

Mum shook her head. "No. Dad's at work all day, and you're both at school, and so am I three days a week. A dog would get really lonely."

Ben sighed and nodded, so Mum went on quickly. "I gave the Cat Rescue Centre a ring this morning. They've got some kittens at the moment, they said, and they're ready for new homes now."

Olivia jumped up, almost upsetting her pasta into her lap. "Let's go!"

"Livvy, sit down!" Mum laughed. "The centre's not even open right now. And anyway, before we can go and choose a kitten, we have to have a home visit. To check that we're going to be suitable owners."

Olivia sat down, staring back at Mum worriedly. "Suitable? What does that mean? Do we have to know loads about cats? I only know a bit. But I've got lots of books about cats, and we could look things up on the computer..."

"Slow down!" Dad patted her shoulder. "It's OK. They're just going to want to check that our road isn't too busy. And that we're happy to put a cat flap in the kitchen door, that kind of thing."

"*And* that we don't have children who won't know how to behave around a cat," Mum said, eyeing Ben grimly. "A lady from the centre is coming to see us this evening, and we'll all have to show her that we're *sensible*, Benjamin Williams."

Ben scowled, and Olivia looked at him warily. Ben wasn't sensible at all. In fact, he was the least sensible person Olivia had ever met.

How were they ever going to convince the lady from the Rescue Centre that they were the right owners for a kitten?

"I'll give you this week's pocket money," Olivia said desperately.

Ben raised one eyebrow.

"And my Saturday sweets too! But you have to promise to be on your absolute best behaviour. Actually, don't even talk! Or – or move!"

Ben zipped his lips with his fingers,

and smirked at her, but Olivia wasn't sure she could trust him.

"Oh, there's the doorbell! Shall we go and answer it, or let Mum?" Olivia twisted her fingers together nervously. She so wanted to make a good impression.

"Mmmpfl." Ben made a strange grunting noise, and Olivia stared at him.

He shrugged. "Well, you said not to talk!"

"That doesn't mean make stupid noises! If she asks you a question you have to say something."

"Something."

"Fine, I'm keeping my pocket money." Olivia marched down the stairs feeling furious. If Ben managed

139

to mess this up, she was never going to forgive him. Ben followed her, sniggering.

Mum was just answering the door to a friendly-looking lady in a Rescue Centre fleece.

"Hi. I'm Debbie, from the Cat Rescue Centre."

"Thanks for coming. I'm Emma and this is my husband, John, and this is Olivia and Ben." Mum led Debbie into the living room, and Olivia and Ben followed behind. Dad went to put the kettle on.

"It seems like a fairly quiet area." Debbie made a note on the sheet she was holding. "Not too many cars."

"Lots of people around here have cats," Olivia put in hopefully.

Mum laughed. "And Olivia is friends with all of them!"

Olivia perched nervously on the edge of the sofa. Ben was sitting on the sofa arm, and for once he didn't look as though he was planning anything silly. Olivia crossed her fingers. "Are there really kittens at the Rescue Centre right now?" she asked Debbie shyly.

Debbie nodded. "Two litters, actually. One's mostly ginger and white, and the other litter are a smoky grey. They're all really sweet."

Olivia's eyes shone as she imagined sitting on the sofa, just like she was now, but with a tiny grey kitten purring on her lap.

Debbie went through a long list of

questions, checking how much time the kitten would be left alone, and that Olivia's mum knew they'd have to pay for vet's bills. Olivia could see the list if she leaned over, and it mostly had ticks in the boxes. Hopefully Debbie would say yes!

Just as Debbie was handing Mum some leaflets about pet insurance and flea treatments, Dad came in with a tray of tea. He passed the cups round, then he sat down on the sofa next to Olivia. There was a sudden, very loud, very rude noise, and Dad jumped up, his face scarlet.

Ben practically fell off the sofa arm he was laughing so much, and Olivia pulled out a whoopee cushion from behind Dad.

"Ben!" Mum sounded horrified.

"I'd forgotten it was there, sorry," Ben said, but he didn't look very sorry at all.

Olivia looked over at Debbie, her eyes starting to burn with tears. Did having a stupid, rude big brother mean no kitten?

But Debbie was giggling. "I haven't seen one of those in ages. My brother used to do that all the time." Then she looked serious. "A kitten really is a big responsibility, though. And everyone in the family has to be prepared to help care for it properly." She was staring at Ben, who looked embarrassed.

"I will look after it, I promise," he muttered.

Debbie nodded. "Right then." She signed her name in swirly letters across the bottom of the form. "You can come and choose your kitten tomorrow!"

Chapter Two

Olivia doodled on her reading record book, trying to think of the best name for a beautiful little grey kitten, or perhaps a sweet gingery one. She quite liked Esmeralda, herself. But then Dad had said at breakfast that it had to be a name that they didn't mind yelling down the garden to get the kitten to come in for tea. Olivia giggled.

She couldn't really see Ben shouting, "Es-mer-al-da!"

Fluffy? Smoky? Whiskers? None of them sounded quite right. Olivia scowled down at the picture she was drawing. A kitten with big, sad eyes, just waiting for her to come and bring him home. She wished they'd been able to go to the Rescue Centre yesterday, straight after Debbie had approved them, but Mum said they needed to get everything ready first, and Olivia supposed she was right. They didn't even have a food bowl!

Lucie elbowed her in the ribs. "Mr Jones has got his eye on you, Olivia!"

Olivia straightened up and tried to look as though she was listening. She loved history usually, but today she couldn't think of anything except kittens. They were going to the pet shop after school to get everything, and then on to the Rescue Centre!

The kitten finished his bowl of biscuits and licked his paw, swiping it across his nose and ears. Then he trotted over to the wire front of the pen and stood up on his hind paws, his front claws scraping on the wire. He scrabbled at it for a moment, hoping that someone might come and open it for him. Sometimes the Rescue Centre staff came to play with the kittens, when they weren't too busy. But maybe they wouldn't, now that it was only him.

He unhooked his claws, and pattered sadly back to the cushion on the shelf in the corner. It was too big for just him – until yesterday, three small grey kittens had shared it, and now when he curled up he was lost in the middle. He missed his sisters. Even though the centre was kept warm, he still felt chilly all on his own.

"The kittens are this way." Debbie smiled at Olivia and Ben, and their mum and dad. "You haven't changed your minds then? You'd still like one?" she teased.

"Yes!" Olivia nodded so hard her bunches shook up and down. "And we've got a cat basket and a litter tray and a grooming brush and some toys and two bowls!"

Debbie laughed. "All you need is the kitten then! Come on." She led the way down the corridor, which was lined with wire-fronted enclosures. They were full of cats, all watching as Olivia walked past. She blinked, feeling suddenly sad. It wasn't that the little pens weren't nice – the cats all had a basket and toys, and most of the pens were built with a shelf, so the cats could be high up, where they felt safe. But they weren't a proper home. She wondered how often they got cuddled or stroked.

"We do take them all out every day. At least once," Debbie said quietly.

Olivia blinked. How had Debbie known what she was thinking?

"I know it doesn't look very cosy, but it's better than being out in the cold." Debbie sighed. "I'd like to take them all home, but I already have five cats... I can't really have any more..." She shook herself, and smiled firmly. "Look. The two litters of kittens are in the large pens down this side."

"Oh…" Olivia crouched down in front of the wire pen.

Four ginger kittens were bombing around, chasing each other round a scratching post and up on to a shelf where a white cat, who Olivia guessed was their mother, was trying to sleep. They scrambled over her – she looked as though she was used to it by now, her ears didn't even twitch – and then jumped down and did it all over again.

"Goodness," Mum muttered. "They're very energetic, aren't they?"

Olivia looked up at her anxiously. She hoped Mum wasn't changing her mind. "We're only going to have one," she pointed out, her voice a little squeaky with worry. "They only look bouncy because there's so many of them."

Debbie nodded. "Kittens are very energetic, but Olivia's right. Just one won't be quite so crazy. Look, we've got just one grey kitten left in the pen a little further down, he's a bit calmer."

Olivia had been so excited seeing the gorgeous ginger kittens that she'd almost forgotten there was one more.

"There were three in this litter, but two of them were rehomed yesterday. I think this little one's feeling a bit lonely." Debbie beckoned them along the corridor to the enclosure, where a small grey kitten was stretched out on his sleeping shelf, licking a paw and looking sad. He glanced up as Olivia and her family came closer, and Olivia laughed delightedly. His round green eyes gave him a permanent surprised look, and he had a dark smudge on his tail – almost as though someone had flicked a black paintbrush at him.

The kitten jumped down from his sleeping shelf, and pattered over to the wire front of the pen.

"He's so beautiful, Mum," Olivia whispered. "Look at him! He's so cute, with his little smudgy tail!"

"He is very sweet," Mum agreed.

The kitten mewed hopefully. He liked Debbie, and he knew she usually came to feed him and fuss over him. And he liked the look of the other people too. Maybe they'd pick him up. They might even take him away with them. Someone had taken his sisters, so why not him?

"Where did he come from?" Dad asked. "You don't have his mum as well, like the other kittens?"

Debbie shook her head, and sighed. "No…" She glanced at Ben and Olivia, as though she didn't want to upset them. "These kittens were abandoned. A lady out for a walk by the canal found them. Someone had just left them in a cardboard box."

Olivia stared at the kitten, who was pawing hopefully at the wire. How could someone just have abandoned him?

"They were lucky to be found so quickly," Debbie added. "They were only two weeks old; they would have died if they'd been left much longer without food." She patted Olivia's arm, seeing how upset she was. "But the good thing about it is that the kittens were bottle-fed, which means they're super-friendly. This one is a little love. He wants to be cuddled all the time."

"Can we have him?" Olivia turned round. "Ben, don't you think he's gorgeous?"

"I suppose. The ginger ones were really fun, but he looks friendly, too," Ben said.

"Let's get him out so you can give him a stroke," Debbie suggested.

"Oh, yes please…" Olivia gazed through the wire at the kitten. He was scrabbling at it now, looking as though he liked the idea too. Debbie opened the front of the pen, and laughed as he scampered out before she could catch him.

The kitten skidded to a stop in front of Olivia's feet, and glanced up, suddenly shy. He looked at Olivia sideways, obviously wondering who she was and if she was friendly.

Olivia stretched out her fingers to him, and he sniffed them, and then rubbed the side of his face up and down her hand. "Ahhh. Do you think I could pick him up?" she asked Debbie.

"Give it a try. Don't worry if he wriggles away, he'll probably be a bit excited."

But the kitten snuggled happily against Olivia's school jumper, and purred. This was just what he wanted. So much better than being all alone in the pen, and the girl smelled nice.

Olivia stroked him gently behind the ears. His fur was soft and velvety, and he nuzzled a tiny, cold pink nose into her neck, making her giggle. "Oh, listen to him purring! He feels like a little lawn mower!"

The kitten closed his eyes happily, and kneaded his paws into Olivia's shoulder.

Debbie smiled. "He's definitely taken to you."

Olivia's eyes glowed as she looked up at her parents, kitten paws tangled in her jumper. "Please can we have him?"

"But what about the ginger ones?" Ben grumbled, but then he stroked the top of the kitten's head. "I guess he is quite cute," he admitted.

Dad nodded, smiling. "So what are we going to call him then?"

In the end, the name was obvious. Smudge just fitted. Olivia's mum suggested Alfie, and Ben wanted to call him after his favourite footballer, but Smudge just looked like Smudge.

He fitted into the house too. Debbie had said that he was already house-trained. She'd also explained that Smudge had had all his vaccinations, and was safe to go outside, but it would be better not to let him out on his own for the first couple of weeks, while he got used to his new home. Dad was glad about that, as it gave him a bit longer to fit the cat flap.

On his first night, Olivia had left Smudge curled up in his new basket.

She'd lined up all his toys next to him, and given him one of her old toy cats in case he was lonely. Then she'd refilled his water bowl, and given him a prawn-flavour cat treat as a bedtime snack.

"Olivia, it's way past your bedtime!" Mum put an arm round her shoulders. "He'll be fine. He's used to the Rescue Centre. I'm sure our kitchen's much nicer than that pen he was in."

Olivia nodded. "Yes, but he doesn't know our house yet, and he doesn't understand what's happening. What if he thinks we're never coming back?"

"Come on. You're not sleeping in the kitchen with him, Livvy."

Olivia sighed and looked back sadly as Mum shooed her out. The light from the hallway gleamed in the kitten's huge eyes. He looked sad too.

Upstairs, Olivia got ready for bed. But she couldn't stop thinking about Smudge, alone in the dark kitchen. Perhaps she should just go and check on him?

Ben was lying on his bed reading, and he glanced up as Olivia went past. "Mum'll hear if you sneak downstairs, Olivia. She always catches me."

Olivia leaned round his bedroom door. "How did you know what I was doing?" she hissed. "I might just have been going to the loo!"

Ben shrugged. "I could tell by the way you were looking at the stairs." He frowned. "Hey, is that Smudge making that noise?"

From downstairs came a faint but pitiful wailing, along with a scratching sound. The noise of kitten claws scrabbling at a kitchen door.

Olivia hung over the banisters, listening to the sad little howls.

Eventually Mum came out of the living room, frowning. "I hope he's all right," she said over her shoulder to Dad. "Oh, Olivia. Is he keeping you awake?"

"Can't we let him come upstairs?" Olivia pleaded. "He sounds so lonely."

Mum sighed and glanced at Dad.

Dad shrugged. "Well, he is house-trained."

"Thank you!" Olivia smiled with delight, and ran down the stairs to open the kitchen door.

Smudge shot out, and she gathered him into her arms, cuddling him against her pyjamas. "Don't worry, Smudge," she whispered. "I'll look after you." She carried him upstairs, and put him down gently on her bed.

Smudge looked around interestedly, and padded up and down Olivia's duvet, inspecting it carefully. Olivia tried not to laugh. He looked so serious. Then he marched over to her pillow, curled himself up in the hollow between the pillow and the duvet, and went to sleep.

Chapter Three

Smudge had only been there a few days, but Olivia's house was definitely his home now. He had explored every possible hole and hiding place, and got stuck in several of them. But Olivia or Ben or their parents were always there to rescue him. Except for today. Dad was at work, Olivia and Ben had gone to school that morning, and as it was

Thursday their mum had to go into school to work too. Smudge was all on his own for the first time, and he didn't like it. He wandered around the house, his tail twitching. He'd already been into every room that was open, and he knew that no one was there, but he kept hoping that maybe if he looked again he would find somebody.

He padded back into the kitchen, and sniffed hopefully at the door. Olivia and Ben had taken him out into the garden when they got home from school yesterday. It had been his first taste of the outside world, and his ears flickered back and forth as he remembered watching the birds, and chasing after the little jingly ball that Olivia had rolled along the patio.

There it was, in the corner by the kitchen cupboards. Smudge trotted over and patted the ball with one paw. It rolled along, the little bell jingling, and he pounced on it. The ball slid along the polished tiles, and so did Smudge, rolling over on to his back, wriggling and clawing at it. But then the ball slid away from his paws and stopped against the kitchen table leg, and it wasn't as much fun any more.

Grumpily, Smudge lay there on his back, licking his paws. He'd already had quite a long sleep in the recycling box on the kitchen counter. (Ben had emptied it that morning, and it was just the right size for Smudge to feel cosy in, much better than his basket.) Now he wanted someone to play with.

Perhaps by the time he got upstairs, Olivia would be back in her bedroom? He trotted through to the hallway and started to struggle up the stairs.

He was big enough to climb them, but it was an effort, and he had to scrabble and heave himself up each step. He sat down for a little while at the top of the stairs, his sides heaving, and then he crept along the landing and nosed his way round Olivia's door.

She wasn't there. The room was empty.

Smudge crept under Olivia's bed. He picked his way between two tottering piles of books, and pounced on the flex of Olivia's hair-dryer. Then, yawning, he snuggled himself inside her gym bag. He liked small spaces, and climbing the stairs had worn him out. When he woke up, surely they would all be back?

"I can't believe it's only lunchtime," Olivia muttered, checking her watch for the hundredth time.

"Are you missing Smudge?" Lucie grinned at her.

Olivia nodded. "It's the first time we've left him alone all day. I really hope he's OK. He nearly climbed out of the living-room window yesterday. I caught him just as he was sticking his head out."

"He still isn't allowed out then? Isn't he old enough?"

"He's ten weeks, so he could go outside, but Debbie said it's best if we wait until we've had him a bit longer before letting him out on his own. It already feels like he's been with us for ages, though. He isn't shy or nervous at all." Then she shook her head. "Except for yesterday, when we took Smudge into the garden with us, and Ben got him with his water pistol. He *said* it was an accident, but I don't know…"

Lucie sighed. "I'm so jealous. I love Tiger, but he's really old and just sleeps all day. Can I come and see Smudge soon?" she asked hopefully.

Olivia nodded. She was desperate to show off how gorgeous Smudge was. "Do you want to come to tea tomorrow? Mum's doing playground duty, we could go and ask her."

They ran over to Olivia's mum, who was turning the end of a skipping rope for a bunch of year one girls. "Mum, can Lucie come to tea tomorrow? She really wants to see Smudge."

Mum frowned. "Oh, not Friday, Lucie, sorry. Ben's already invited Rob. I'll ask your mum about popping over at the weekend," she suggested, and Lucie nodded, looking pleased, but Olivia was frowning.

"Rob's coming? To tea? Mum, does

he have to? Ben always plays up when Rob's round, they'll be awful! They might upset Smudge!"

"I'm sure they won't, Olivia. Oh dear! Up you get, Sinead!" One of the year ones had tripped over the rope, and Mum went to pick her up.

Olivia sighed, and glanced at Lucie. "I bet they will. You know what Ben's like. And with Rob there he's three times as bad. I'll just have to keep Smudge with me the whole time."

"Smudge! Where are you, puss?" As soon as Olivia got home from school, she dropped her bag, pulled off her coat, and dashed upstairs to search for him.

Maybe he was having a sleep on her bed? As she pushed her bedroom door wide open, there was a little mew and Smudge wriggled out from under her bed. A pile of books toppled over as he shot out and scrambled into her lap. Olivia giggled. "Mum's right, I really do need to tidy up, especially if you're going to go exploring under there. Those books nearly squashed your tail!" She settled down to do her homework with Smudge purring on her knee. When she'd finished she carried him downstairs, and wandered into the kitchen to talk to Mum. Ben was out in the garden building a den in the apple tree.

"Mum, does Rob have to come to tea tomorrow?"

Mum looked up from the saucepan she was stirring. "Well, yes. It's all arranged. What's the matter, Livvy?"

Olivia shrugged. "I don't want him to…" she whispered. "He does stupid stuff, and he makes Ben do stupid stuff too. They always get into trouble."

Mum sighed. "I know they're a bit naughty. But Rob is Ben's best friend. Can't you just stay out of their way tomorrow, love?"

"But what if they upset Smudge? Can I take him up to my room tomorrow to keep him out of their way too?"

Mum looked at her seriously for a moment, and shook her head. "Olivia, Ben wants to show Smudge off to Rob. I know you really love Smudge, and he's taken to you so well, but he's not just yours, sweetheart. He's Ben's kitten as well."

Olivia nodded miserably. She knew Mum was right, but it didn't help. Smudge *felt* like he was her kitten, and she didn't want the boys anywhere near him.

"Hello, Smudge!" Olivia's dad walked in, and tickled the kitten under the chin.

Then Ben flung open the kitchen door, and stomped muddy footprints across the floor. "Is it dinnertime yet?"

"Shoes off!" Mum grabbed him. "And then it is, yes."

Olivia rolled her eyes at Mum. "You see?" she muttered. She let Smudge down to the floor and went to help pass the bowls of pasta round.

"What?" Ben asked, as he hopped around taking off his trainers.

Olivia folded her arms. "I just don't think it's a good idea for you to have Rob over tomorrow. Not when we've only had Smudge for three days. Rob'll probably get Smudge to … to climb trees or something. You always do stupid things with him! Like that time you dug a tunnel and pulled up all Dad's daffodil bulbs!"

Ben shook his head. "That *so* isn't fair! For a start, we didn't know they were there! And anyway, Rob loves cats. He's been asking his mum and dad for one for ages. He can't wait to meet Smudge."

"Oh…" Olivia muttered.

"Actually, where is Smudge?" Mum asked.

Olivia looked down, expecting to see him by her feet, hoping to be fed. But he wasn't there.

"I don't know." Olivia went to look in the hallway, but then there was a worried little meow from somewhere on the other side of the kitchen.

Mum frowned. "Where on earth is he?"

The meowing got louder.

"I think he's behind the cooker!" Ben said suddenly.

"But it's still hot from cooking dinner!" Mum cried.

Olivia dashed over to the cooker. "Smudge, come out of there!"

But Smudge only mewed louder.

"He's stuck," Olivia muttered, crouching down and trying to reach behind the cooker. "Ow, and it's hot. I can't get to him. I think he got trapped and now he can't turn round!"

Dad shook his head. "What is it with that kitten? The smaller the space, the more he likes it. I'll have to pull it out a bit."

He dragged the cooker out from the wall, and Smudge darted out and ran to Olivia. He was trembling, and covered in dust balls – he looked even furrier than usual.

Mum shook her head. "I don't think Smudge needs the boys to get him into trouble, Olivia. He can manage it perfectly well on his own!"

Chapter Four

After school on Friday, Olivia ran into the house ahead of Rob and Ben, looking for Smudge.

The little grey kitten slipped round the living-room door, mewing excitedly, and purred as she picked him up. Olivia stroked him lovingly, and then took a step back as Rob came over to her. She was used to Rob racing around the playground with Ben, chasing people and getting into trouble. She wasn't sure he knew how to be careful with a kitten.

"Hey! He's really cute!"

Olivia nodded slowly.

"Can I stroke him? Will he mind?" Even Rob's voice was gentler than usual.

"Um, OK..." Olivia looked on anxiously, but Rob tickled Smudge behind the ears – his favourite place, and Smudge purred and wriggled so that Olivia had to hand him over, letting him fasten his claws in Rob's school sweater.

"He likes you!" Ben commented. "Come on, bring him up to my room." He grabbed Smudge's favourite jingly ball and a squeaky mouse.

"But…" Olivia watched as the boys thundered up the stairs, taking Smudge with them. She started to run after them, but Mum called her back. "Leave them on their own, Olivia."

"But they've taken Smudge up there. What are they going to do with him?"

Mum laughed. "Just play with him, like you do! Rob seems to really like him. Come on, Livvy. Come and make some chocolate-chip cookies with me, we can have them after tea."

Olivia sighed. She supposed Mum was right. Maybe she was just feeling jealous because Smudge seemed to like Rob.

They were in the middle of cutting out the biscuits, when Ben and Rob and Smudge came down to watch TV.

Olivia looked at Smudge carefully, but he seemed to be all right. The boys hadn't trimmed his whiskers, or painted him blue, or done any of the other stupid things she'd been imagining.

A little later, Ben came into the kitchen. "Are the cookies ready yet? They smell fantastic."

"The first trayful are nearly done, but they're for after tea, Ben! We're having fish fingers. And I can see you stealing the chocolate!" Mum waved a spoon at him, as Ben popped a handful of choc drops into his mouth, grinning.

"Where's Smudge?" Olivia asked anxiously.

"Sitting on the sofa with Rob – calm down, Olivia! He's fine. Rob thinks he's great."

Olivia stared out of the kitchen door, hoping Smudge might come in to see her. But he stayed with Rob.

Smudge yawned, and stretched out his paws. Rob was stroking him very nicely, but he wanted to go and see what Olivia was doing. He hadn't seen her all day, and he wanted her to play with him. And he was hungry. There were food smells coming from the kitchen, good fishy smells, he thought. He stood up sleepily, getting ready to jump off Rob's lap.

Rob looked down. "Where are you going, Smudge?" He tickled him under the chin and Smudge purred. Maybe he wouldn't go just yet.

"Ben's so lucky," Rob murmured gently. "I wish I had a kitten like you." He sighed, and picked up his school bag from the floor, rooting around in it.

Smudge peered over, and stuck his nose in. It smelled good.

Rob laughed. "I'm just looking for my Polos, but I don't think they're good for cats. Oh, I bet I know what you can smell. My leftover ham sandwich." He laughed again as Smudge stuck his whole head in the bag. "Where are you going?"

Smudge could smell the delicious ham at the bottom of the bag, and he wriggled all the way in.

"Hey, Ben's going to think I'm taking you home." Rob grinned. But then his smile faded a little. Smudge popped his

185

head out of the bag, licking round his jaws hopefully. "There isn't any more, Smudge, sorry."

The little kitten yawned widely, and ducked back into the bag, curling up at the bottom and closing his eyes.

Rob shook his head. "I can't believe you're asleep in my school bag." He stared at Smudge thoughtfully and sighed. "I really could take you home…"

"Mrs Williams…"

"Oh, hello, Rob. Do you want to help with the cookies?"

Rob was standing by the kitchen door, looking shifty. "Um. No. I have to go home. Um, I feel sick."

"Oh dear!" Olivia's mum put down the tray of biscuits, and hurried over to him.

Ben and Olivia stared at Rob in surprise. "You don't look ill," Ben said.

"Has it just suddenly come over you?" Olivia's mum asked. "Are you hot?"

Rob backed away from her, and nodded. "Yes. And I feel *really* sick. Please can I ring my mum?"

"Of course." She handed him the phone. "You poor thing."

Rob took the phone out into the hallway, and they could hear him explaining urgently to his mum.

"He does sound very upset, poor Rob," Olivia's mum said anxiously.

"He was fine ten minutes ago," Ben muttered.

Olivia frowned. "I bet he's broken something. And he doesn't want to get into trouble. Did he mess anything up in your room?"

"Don't be silly, Olivia. The boys have just been watching TV. How could he have broken anything?" Mum glared at her crossly. "You mustn't be mean."

"She's coming." Rob stood at the

kitchen door, holding out the phone to Olivia's mum.

Rob's mum arrived a few minutes later, and Olivia's mum chatted to her, while Rob lurked impatiently by the door. "I'm really sorry. I don't think it's anything he's eaten – we hadn't even had tea."

Rob's mum shook her head. "It's probably just something going round – I only hope he hasn't given it to Ben and Olivia. At least he's got the weekend to recover. Anyway, I'd better get him home. Thank you for having him!"

Rob darted into the living room and came out carrying his school bag. He was holding it against his tummy, hunching over, and his mum looked at him worriedly. "Oh dear, you do look as though you might be sick. Come on, let's get you home." She led him down the path to the car.

Mum closed the door and hurried into the kitchen. "I'd forgotten about the fish fingers with all of that going on; I'm afraid they might be a bit crispy..."

"Can Smudge have one of Rob's ones?" Olivia asked. "I bet he'd love a fish finger." Then she jumped up suddenly. "Where is Smudge?" she asked, her voice a little panicky. "I haven't seen him in ages. Rob was cuddling him in the living room."

"Perhaps Rob shut the living-room door?" Mum suggested, as she served up tea. "He's probably stuck in there."

But the living-room door was open and there was no Smudge on the sofa, or hiding behind it to leap out at Olivia as she searched around. She darted upstairs to look in her room.

"Smudge! Smudge! Mum, he's not in there, and I've checked upstairs, and I can't find him anywhere!" Olivia ran back into the kitchen.

Ben was sitting at the table eating a huge pile of fish fingers – his and Rob's. "He'll be under your bed or something. I'll come and help you look." But Smudge wasn't in either of their rooms, and he hadn't climbed into the bath and got stuck. He wasn't in the airing cupboard on the towels either.

"Could he have got out somehow?" Ben asked when they came back downstairs.

Mum frowned. "I'm sure all the windows were shut. After he nearly got out yesterday I was a bit worried he might try that again."

Olivia nodded. "I checked all the windows this morning, before we went to school."

Mum sighed. "Smudge must be hiding somewhere, like he always does. He'll pop out at us in a minute, I'm sure."

Olivia turned to Ben, her hands on her hips. "Did you and Rob let him outside?"

Ben stared at her, wide-eyed. "He was just watching TV with us, Olivia. We didn't even *go* out, so how's it our fault suddenly?"

"I bet that's why Rob wanted to go home." Olivia sat down on a chair as her knees suddenly felt shaky. "He was scared he was going to get into trouble. You let him out. I can't believe you'd do that!" she yelled.

"Olivia!" Mum warned. "You're just jumping to conclusions."

"We didn't let him out!" Ben stood up angrily. "How many times do I have to say it?" He stomped out of the kitchen, muttering. "I'm going to look for him upstairs. He must be here somewhere."

Olivia slumped on her chair, feeling tears welling up in her eyes. However much Ben denied it, she was sure the boys had let Smudge get out – either by accident, or as part of some stupid game. Smudge was so little! He'd only been outside once, and he'd had her and Ben there to make sure he didn't escape from the garden, or get himself stuck somewhere. Just thinking of all the places where he might hurt himself made her feel sick.

Chapter Five

Smudge woke up, and was surprised to find that everything was dark, and the bag was bumping around. The little kitten swayed from side to side, mewing with fright. Where was Olivia? Why was he stuck in here? He needed Olivia to let him out!

"Hey, ssshhh. I'm going to get you out of there."

The bag opened, and Smudge could see Rob peering inside. He gave a soft little mew. This wasn't right. He had thought that Olivia would come and find him. He cowered back against the bottom of the bag, and hissed as Rob tried to open it up a bit more. The boy had been kind before, stroking and cuddling him, and feeding him sandwiches, but now Smudge was confused, and he wanted Olivia.

"Hey, Smudge. Don't you want to get out? Come and see my bedroom," Rob said, gently reaching in to pick up the kitten.

Smudge spat crossly as a warning, and when Rob didn't take his hand away, he clawed at it, hard.

"Ow!" Rob sat back, sucking at the bleeding scratch. Then he sighed. "OK. I suppose I'd scratch if I got shut up in a bag and bounced around all over the place. Maybe I'd better get you something else to eat." He smiled at Smudge. "You liked that ham sandwich, didn't you?"

Smudge saw him stand up.

"I'll go and see what's in the fridge, but I might be a while. Mum still thinks I'm sick, so I'll have to wait till she's not looking. Back soon. Here, you can play with this ball, it's got spikes, look! That'd be fun, wouldn't it? See you in a minute, Smudge."

The bedroom door clicked, and Smudge waited, his heart thumping. Had the boy gone? Was it safe to come out?

Slowly, cautiously, he wriggled out of the bag.

"I can't find him anywhere." Ben was standing in the doorway, and his voice had changed. He wasn't angry any more, he sounded frightened.

"I told you so!" Olivia swiped a hand across her eyes. "You must have opened a window, or let him out of the kitchen door, or something!"

"We didn't! You and Mum were in the kitchen the whole time, how could we let him out of here?"

"Ben's right, Olivia, you're not being fair."

"Even if Ben didn't let him out, his stupid friend did!" Olivia sobbed. "And now Smudge is lost!"

"I didn't let him out, I promise I didn't, and Rob didn't either. He would have said if something had happened." Ben's voice was shaking now.

"Both of you calm down. Olivia, try

199

and stop crying, sweetheart, it's only making you feel worse. Come on. We'll all do another proper search round the house. Look at yesterday, when Smudge got himself stuck behind the oven! He's around somewhere, I'm sure of it."

Olivia shook her head. "Then why can't we hear him? If he was here and stuck, he'd be meowing, Mum. Wouldn't he?"

Mum got up. "Maybe you're right. If Smudge was shut in somewhere, we'd hear him. We'd better go and check outside. Maybe there's a window open that we've missed."

"I told you!" Olivia wailed. "Rob let him out, he must have done."

Even Ben was looking less certain now. "Rob wouldn't just let him out –

I told him Smudge wasn't allowed outside on his own yet..."

They hurried out into the garden, calling and calling, but apart from next-door's cat, Lily, who looked very curiously at them, the garden was empty. It was starting to get dark, and cold. Olivia shivered, thinking of Smudge outside in the chilly wind.

"What about the garden shed?" Mum suggested, trying to think of places a kitten might find interesting. "Could he have squeezed himself in there somehow?"

The shed door was tightly shut, but they checked anyway. And under the patio furniture, and behind the pile of flower pots, and even up the cherry tree.

Smudge was nowhere to be found.

"You two stay here, I'll just go and ask Sally next door if she's seen him," Mum said. "Why don't you go and have another look inside?"

"I'm sorry I said you let him out," Olivia muttered, as they peered behind the sofa. "I know you wouldn't really."

"Do you think he'll be all right?"

Ben asked miserably. "I just don't see where he can be!"

Olivia stood up again, and went to check behind the curtains, but then she stopped. "Rob forgot his lunchbox," she said slowly, pointing at a Star Wars lunchbox down by the side of the sofa. "And a load of his books, look. His reading record and everything…"

Ben frowned. "Why would he take all that stuff out of his bag?"

"His bag… He was carrying it in a funny way." Olivia stared at Ben, her eyes wide. "Ben, he didn't let Smudge out, he *stole* him! Rob put Smudge in his school bag and took him home!"

"Don't be stupid," Ben said, but he was chewing his thumbnail worriedly. "He wouldn't… What's he going to do, hide Smudge in his room? I know he really wanted a pet, but he wouldn't steal our cat…"

"I bet you he did," Olivia told him grimly. She heard the sound of the key in the lock, and rushed out into the hallway. "Mum! We think we know where Smudge is!"

Chapter Six

Smudge gazed around the room. He had no idea where he was, but he knew this wasn't home and he wanted to get away. His ears were laid back, listening for footsteps. But no one was coming. He had to get out and find Olivia. He shook his head, feeling dazed from bumping around in the bag. His nose was still full of the smell of ham sandwich, and the musty scent of the inside of the bag, but there was something else…

The window was open! Smudge's eyes widened a little.

Rob's bed was pushed up against the wall. If he could jump on to that, it was only a little climb to the windowsill. But the bed was very high up. Much higher than the steps on the stairs he'd struggled with. Smudge glanced anxiously round at the door. He was sure the boy would be back soon. He had to be quick. With a huge effort, he ran at the bed, hooking his claws into the duvet cover and scrabbling upwards furiously. From the top of the bed it didn't look such a small climb to the windowsill after all, but Rob had nice long curtains. Smudge raced up them, his heart hammering, leaving a pattern of little hooked loops all the way up. And then he scrambled up on to the windowsill.

He peered out of the open window, his nose twitching, trying to see where to go next. But below him was only a straight wall down to the garden. Smudge teetered on the edge of the window, his tail flicking anxiously back and forth. He had to get out, and this was the only way. He edged a little further, on to the outside windowsill. He could see all the way along the garden, and he was sure that if he could get down there, he could find his way back to Olivia somehow. But it was a long way to jump… He paced up and down, mewing pitifully. He was cold, out there on the windowsill. The sky was darkening, and there was a chill wind ruffling his fur. It shook the branches of the tree in the corner of the garden, and they kept tapping against the wall and scraping the windowsill.

Smudge crouched on the windowsill, shivering, and watching the twigs brushing against the wall. It was the only way down, but the branches were like thin little fingers. He had never climbed a tree, and certainly never climbed *down* one.

Suddenly, Smudge whipped round. He could hear the door handle turning. He had to go now! He sprang on to the nearest branch that looked strong enough to hold him, and mewed with fright as it wobbled and dipped underneath him. He clung on desperately, digging his claws into the bark, and wailed as a gust of wind shook the tree again.

He scrabbled his way along the branch towards the tree trunk, and skidded and bumped down to the fence, where he perched, mewing with fright. It was a very narrow fence, but at least it wasn't shaking – or not as much as the tree had been.

Smudge teetered, trying to work out which way to jump. Back into the garden? But then the boy might come and find him. So, down the other side of the fence? There was long grass down there that looked soft enough to jump on to. But he had no idea where the alley went, or if it would lead back to Olivia. There were only a few battered-looking garages.

He jumped, bouncing down the side of the fence, and landing in a flurry of paws on the soft grass. Now where should he go?

"Yes, Rob's here, I'll just get him, Ben."

Ben put his hand over the phone

receiver and nodded to Olivia and Mum. "He's coming."

Olivia sat forward on the sofa, trying to listen, and Ben rolled his eyes and pressed the speakerphone button. Rob's voice echoed out into the room.

"What is it?" He sounded jumpy and worried.

"Where's Smudge?" Ben demanded.

"What do you mean?"

"He knows!" Olivia hissed. Rob was trying to sound as though he didn't understand, but he wasn't very good at it.

"We found all your stuff. You took him away in your school bag, didn't you?" Ben said angrily.

"I'm sorry..." Rob muttered finally. "It was all a mistake. Smudge was sniffing around my bag, and then he climbed in and went to sleep. I just wanted to have him for a bit to see what it would be like…"

"You stole him!" Olivia yelled down the phone. "Bring him back now!"

There was silence. Then Rob whispered, "I can't…"

"What do you mean, you can't?" Ben asked.

"He's gone." Rob sounded almost like he was crying.

"You've *lost* him!" Olivia cried.

"I think he got out of my bedroom window," Rob gulped. "He must have done. I searched my whole room, and he just wasn't anywhere. I'm sorry."

Mum reached out for the phone. "Rob, can you get your mother for me, please."

Olivia didn't even hear as her mum and Rob's tried to sort out what was going on. She was slumped on the sofa, her hands squashed into her eyes to stop herself from crying.

Eventually Mum ended the call, and put one arm round Olivia, and one round Ben.

"It looks like Rob did take Smudge," she said slowly. "His mum said she couldn't believe he'd do something so stupid. He hadn't told her what had happened. She's really sorry."

"What are we going to do?" Olivia wailed. "Can we go round to Rob's house and look for Smudge?"

"Rob's dad just came home, and he's going out to look, and ask all the neighbours," Mum explained. "I don't think there's much point in us going over there, it's almost dark. Rob's mum said he thinks Smudge must have been gone for about half an hour, he could have got away down the road."

"But it's so cold," Olivia whispered. "Smudge is out there all on his own!"

Chapter Seven

Smudge was still hiding in the long grass, wondering what to do. He was dreadfully hungry. If he was at home, he was sure it would be teatime. A bowl of crunchy biscuits, or perhaps some of the meaty stuff he really liked. The thought of food made him more determined. He had to go home. He crept out of the clump of grass, and looked around the alleyway worriedly. He had no idea if he was close to Olivia's house or not.

Perhaps he could call for Olivia? But then, he was still very close to the house. What if that boy heard him?

He took a few steps down the alley, his fur prickling. The air felt strange, and it was making him edgy. He carried on, hoping desperately that he would see some sign of Olivia. Wouldn't she come and look for him? Now he was further away from Rob's house, he risked mewing hopefully. But no one was around to hear him.

A large raindrop landed suddenly on his nose, and he jumped back in surprise. It was followed by another and another, and in seconds Smudge's fur was soaked and clinging to him. The rain was followed by a strange eerie flash that seemed to split the dark sky and then a rolling boom of thunder. Smudge shot across the alley to the tumbledown garages, looking for a place to hide. They were all locked up, but he spotted a hole, where a brick had come loose, and squeezed himself inside. There was another crash of thunder. Startled, he jumped back, bumping into a pile of boxes and paint tins, which fell clattering all around him.

Smudge scampered away with a terrified squeak. When he looked back, he saw that a heavy wooden box had fallen right in front of his hole. He was trapped.

He sprang forward, frantically mewing and clawing at the box, but it was far too heavy for him to move.

At last he stopped scrabbling, and sat back, exhausted. He wove his way through the dusty darkness, round the piles of boxes and bikes and all sorts of rubbish that was stored in the garage, hoping to find another hole. But he couldn't find even the tiniest gap.

Miserably he settled down on a pile of old dust sheets. It was cold, and he was starving, and he wanted to be on Olivia's lap on the sofa. Sadly, he snuffled himself to sleep.

"Look at the rain," Olivia whispered, peering out of the living-room window.

Mum came up behind her, and hugged her. "I'm sure he's tucked himself away somewhere safe. We'll find him tomorrow."

"He's only ever been out in the garden with us." Olivia turned to look at Mum, her eyes wide and worried. "He's never been out in the rain! And the thunder's so scary, he must be terrified."

"Like you," Ben muttered from her doorway. But he didn't seem to be putting much effort into teasing her. He sounded too miserable to bother. He came over to the window, and stared at the rain. "Rob's dad phoned just now. He's asked all the neighbours to look out for Smudge, but he had to stop looking and come back inside – he said he couldn't see anything, it was raining so hard."

Their dad came in, carrying the phone. "Olivia, it's Lucie on the phone for you."

Olivia took the phone reluctantly. She wasn't sure whether she wanted to talk to Lucie or not. She desperately wanted to tell someone how angry she was with Rob, but at the same time she didn't want to have to say that Smudge was missing.

"Hi, Olivia! Mum says I can come round to yours tomorrow, if you like. Would that be OK with your mum?"

"I don't know…" Olivia whispered, her eyes prickling with tears.

"Oh, are you going out?" Lucie's voice was disappointed. "I was hoping we could play with Smudge. I really want to see him!"

Olivia sniffed, and then sobbed. "He's gone!"

There was a confused silence on the other end of the line. "You mean, he had to go back to the Rescue Centre?" Lucie said at last.

"No. You know Rob was coming for tea with Ben – he took him."

"Rob Ford stole your kitten?" Lucie sounded as though she didn't quite believe it.

Olivia gave a cross little laugh. "I know it sounds stupid, but he really did! He even owned up to it. But then Smudge tried to get away from him and climbed out of his bedroom window, and now we don't know where he is!"

"What are you going to do?" Lucie whispered in horror.

"We're going to look for him tomorrow – Mum says it's too dark to go round there now. But he could be anywhere, Lucie. And it's a horrible night."

"Can I come and help you look? I bet my mum will come too. The more people the more chance there is we'll spot him," Lucie suggested.

For the first time since she'd realized Smudge was gone, Olivia felt a little bit better. "Would you really help look?"

"Call me tomorrow and let me know when," Lucie told her firmly. "We'll find him."

"OK," Olivia whispered. "Thanks, Lucie. See you in the morning." She put the phone back in its cradle. "Lucie's going to come over and help us look," she explained to Mum and Dad.

Dad nodded. "That's nice of her. Look, I think you should go to bed. You're only sitting here making yourself feel worse. And we want to get up early and go and look for Smudge."

224

Olivia nodded, and went up to her room, but she didn't think she'd be able to get to sleep. And when she did, she was sure she was going to dream about Smudge all night. Smudge lost and all alone, and wondering why she hadn't come to find him.

She lay in her warm bed, listening to the rain drumming on the roof outside her window, and hoping that Smudge was tucked away somewhere safe. But he could be anywhere, she thought worriedly, turning over, and huddling under her duvet. What if they never found him? What would they say to the people from the Rescue Centre? Debbie had said they would call in the next few days to see how they were getting on, and whether Smudge was settling in. They would have to tell her that they had lost him! Or actually, that a stupid, selfish, idiot boy had stolen him.

Olivia thumped her pillow. At least being angry with Rob had stopped her wanting to cry. She wondered if someone could be sent to prison for stealing a kitten. Rob certainly deserved it. Dreamily, she imagined Rob in handcuffs, and herself standing there, with Smudge purring in her arms, watching as the police led him away.

It seemed so real. For a moment, she could hear Smudge purring, she was sure. But it was only the rain, beating against her window.

Chapter Eight

Smudge woke up, shivering. Although he had huddled himself into the pile of dustsheets, it was freezing inside the garage. He felt so cold he could hardly move. At last he stood up gingerly, stretching out his paws and fluffing up his fur to keep himself as warm as possible. He was sure that he was colder because he was so hungry. The last food he'd had was the sandwich in that boy's bag yesterday afternoon, and now he felt horribly empty.

It was getting light. There were dirty, greyish windows at the top of the walls, just under the roof, and a little watery sunshine was fighting its way in. Somehow it made Smudge feel more cheerful, even if it wasn't making him much warmer. In the light he could see that the garage was full of piles of old junk – bits of cars and bikes, piles of pots of paint, and lots of dust. Last night it had just been strange shapes that wobbled when he scurried past them. It was all a lot less scary in the daylight.

He jumped down from his pile of dust sheets, his legs still stiff and achy from the cold, and started to search for a way out. Last night, with the rain pouring down, the garage had at least been a shelter. Now it was stopping him going home to Olivia, and he was determined to escape. Surely now it was lighter he would be able to find another hole somewhere? Smudge made his way along the wall, sniffing and nudging at the concrete blocks.

Edging round the side of a large box, his whiskers twitched hopefully as he spotted a little light coming through a crack at the bottom of the wall. He nosed at it eagerly, and then his whiskers drooped again. It was such a very small gap. But he had to try. The rest of the walls were made from solid concrete blocks, but here one of the blocks seemed to have broken, and it had been patched up with a metal sheet on the outside. If he wriggled into the dark gap between the blocks, there was a tiny hole. Perhaps if he clawed at it for a while, it might give way?

Smudge scrabbled hopefully, his tiny claws making an eerie screeching noise against the rough metal sheet. He scratched and scraped for what seemed like ages, till his claws ached, but when he stopped and pressed his nose against the hole, it didn't seem to have got any bigger at all…

"Olivia! What time is it?" Dad moaned.

"Um, half-past five. You said we'd get up early and go straight round to Rob's!"

"I meant more like seven…" Dad murmured wearily.

"Go back to bed until half-past six,"

Mum added. "We can't go and wake up Rob's family this early."

Olivia sighed. She supposed Mum was right. But she had been lying awake since five, watching her bedroom get lighter and lighter. As soon as it seemed to be light enough to search for a kitten, she had got up.

She mooched back into her room, and lay down on her bed. She wasn't going to be able to go back to sleep. Instead she grabbed a notebook from her bedside table, and started to make a list of things it would be useful to take with them on the search.

A torch, in case they had to look anywhere dark, Olivia thought. Under a shed or something like that. Smudge's favourite snacks. He really liked the little heart-shaped chicken ones. Olivia had done a taste test on five different sorts, and he always went for the chicken ones first. If he was stuck up a tree or anything like that, he would definitely come down for them.

What else? Olivia chewed the end of her pencil. A ladder? She wasn't sure Dad would want to carry one around.

"Oh, you're awake!" Mum put her head round Olivia's door. Olivia gazed up at her. Of course she was! How could she go back to sleep?

"Can I get up?" she asked eagerly.

Mum nodded. "Yes. But we're not going anywhere until you've had some breakfast. Just a quick bowl of cereal, that's all," she added, seeing Olivia was about to moan. "If you eat, you'll be able to hunt for him better."

Olivia dressed quickly, and then ran downstairs to gulp down the bowl of cereal that Mum insisted on. Then she fetched the torch and the snacks, and stood by the front door, waiting impatiently for Mum and Dad and Ben.

"What about Lucie?" she asked Mum, who was putting on her coat.

"I've texted her mum. It's still only seven-thirty, Olivia, I didn't want to get her out of bed. But I've told her where we'll be; she can call my mobile if she and Lucie want to come."

Dad gave an enormous yawn. "Everyone ready?"

They met Rob's dad halfway down Rob's road, crouching down to look under a big wheelie bin.

"No luck yet then?" Mum asked.

He shook his head. "Not yet. But he can't have gone far. I'm really sorry about this. Rob feels terrible. He's looking further up the road with his mum."

So he should! Olivia thought. But being furious with Rob didn't really help.

She and Ben and Mum and Dad set off up the road, calling and peering over fences. Olivia kept shaking the treats, hoping to see a little grey kitten dash eagerly towards her, like he did at home.

Half an hour later, they were back outside Rob's house, and everyone looked rather hopeless. Especially Rob. It seemed as though he'd been crying, and Olivia almost felt sorry for him.

"Not a sign," Dad said, frowning. "And none of the people we asked had spotted him."

"Should we go further? The next street?" Rob's mum asked doubtfully.

"Oh, look!" Mum pointed down the road.

"What is it? Can you see him?" Olivia gasped.

"Sorry, Olivia. It's Lucie, down at the end of the road, with her mum."

Lucie came running up the road as soon as she spotted Olivia. "We'll find him," she promised, seeing her friend's miserable face and hugging her tightly.

"I'm sure we will," her mum agreed, as they reached the little crowd outside Rob's house. "There's lots of us looking now."

Everyone was still discussing where to look next.

"He couldn't still be in your garden, hidden away?" Olivia suggested.

"We looked. We really did," Rob mumbled.

But his mum nodded. "We did, but if Smudge was frightened, he might have hidden himself. Maybe if Ben and Olivia went and called him? It's worth a try, anyway." She led them down the side of the house and into the back garden, and went inside to make some tea for everyone.

"Smudge! Smudge!" Olivia shook the cat treats again and again, and Ben jingled Smudge's favourite ball.

Lucie walked around the garden searching under all the bushes. But Smudge didn't appear. The garden was so quiet and empty.

I don't think we're ever going to find him, Olivia thought, staring sadly at the house. She knew Smudge had been here just last night, but he hadn't left even the tiniest clue. "Is that your window?" she asked Rob, who was lurking on the patio. She could see football stickers on a window that looked desperately high up. Had Smudge really climbed out of there?

Lucie gulped. "That's so high!"

Rob nodded miserably. "I think he must have jumped into that tree."

The girls went over to look at it. It was a plum tree – they could see the odd fruit still left at the top of the branches. It filled the gap between the house and the fence, and some of the branches spilled over the other side.

"What's over there?" Ben asked, trying to scramble up and grab the top of the fence.

"Just some old garages and stuff. There's an alley that runs from the road behind ours," Rob said. "But the fence is really solid. He couldn't have got under it. He must have gone round the side of the house and out the front."

But Olivia stared at the tree and the fence, thoughtfully. "What if he didn't go under the fence? Couldn't he have gone *over* it?"

"Of course not, look how tall it is…" Ben trailed off. "Oh! From the tree!"

Olivia nodded. "How do we get round there?"

Rob lead them round the side of the house, and Ben popped his head through the back door to explain they were going to look in the alleyway.

"We'll just be five minutes," he said quickly, and they vanished into the alley before anyone had time to stop them.

"Why didn't we think of it before?" Rob muttered, as they hurried off. "We just thought he must have gone out the front way."

The alley ran along halfway between Rob's house and the one next door, but they had to go into the next street to get into it. It was very narrow, with a row of tumbledown old garages – and lots of hiding places for a kitten.

"Smudge!" Olivia tore the treats packet open with her teeth, and shook out a handful.

Inside the garage, Smudge was pacing up and down by the hole in the wall. He had to keep trying – he had to get out! He scraped determinedly at the metal sheet, ignoring his sore paws. Then his ears pricked up suddenly as he heard the sound of a familiar voice. Was that Olivia? Had she come to find him? He scrabbled furiously at the wall again, trying to show her where he was.

"Hey, what was that?" Lucie said suddenly. "Something scratching!"

Everyone froze, holding their breath, waiting for the sound again.

"I can't hear anything!" Ben hissed.

"Shh! Listen, there it is again!" Lucie whispered.

Olivia jumped, dropping half the treats on the ground. "I heard it too! It must be him. Smudge, where are you?" she called.

There was silence for a minute, and then a loud, desperate meow.

"It is! It is! Where is he? Smudge, we're coming to find you!" Olivia called, running towards the garages.

Inside the garage, Smudge scrabbled at the metal again. He could hear Olivia! She'd come to find him. Furiously he scraped and scratched, mewing as loudly as he could. He had to make them hear him!

"Which one is it?" Ben asked.

"The one at the end, I think," Rob

said, smiling for the first time that morning. "He must be stuck somehow, he's trying to get out."

Olivia pushed her way past him, and crouched down by the garage wall. "He's here somewhere. Smudge... Smudge..."

A little grey paw suddenly stuck out from a hole in the concrete wall, where it had been patched together.

"He's there! I saw him. Oh, Smudge, we've missed you!" Olivia stroked the grubby little paw. "Look, his claws are all torn where he's been trying to get out." She sniffed, choking back sudden tears.

"How are we going to get him out?" Ben asked. "That hole isn't nearly big enough."

"What about this?" Rob held up a thick stick, which he'd found lying on the grass. "Couldn't we use it to pull that metal away a bit more?" He banged gently on the metal sheet, and the paw shot back inside as Smudge jumped back in fright.

"Don't scare him!" Olivia snapped.

Rob shook his head. "I had to, Olivia. If he was right behind the metal, I might hurt his paws with the stick."

"Oh." Olivia nodded.

Rob hooked the stick into the hole, and pulled. There was a creaking noise, and the thin metal bent a little.

"It's getting bigger! Here, I'll pull too." Ben added his weight to the stick, and Olivia knelt down by the hole.

"Don't be scared, Smudge, you'll be

out of there in a minute."

"There!" Ben said triumphantly. "That must be big enough. Good plan, Rob!"

Inside the garage, Smudge blinked at the hole, his whiskers quivering excitedly. He could hear Olivia. He edged forward, squeezing himself tightly against the concrete block, and suddenly tumbled forward out of the hole, and into Olivia's hands.

"Oh, Smudge, we've been looking everywhere." Olivia snuggled the kitten up against her chin, laughing and crying at the same time.

"Hey! You've found him!" Olivia's dad came running up the alley, with all the others hurrying behind him.

"He's fine," Olivia told them. "Just a bit dirty. He was stuck in that garage."

"We moved that bit of metal," Ben explained. "It was Rob who thought of it."

"But he wouldn't have run off and got stuck if I hadn't taken him first," Rob muttered. "I'll never do anything that stupid again, I promise."

"You're just lucky that you found him," his dad pointed out grimly.

"I know it was all my fault," Rob

muttered. "I said I'm really sorry, Dad."

"I think you'd better give some of your pocket money to the Rescue Centre by way of apology," his mum suggested, and Rob nodded.

Olivia looked over at Rob. "He only did it because he really wants a cat of his own," she murmured.

Rob's dad sighed. "Well, maybe when he proves he can be sensible enough to look after a kitten, he can have one. Which will take a long time!"

Olivia turned to Rob. "Rob, do you want to stroke Smudge too?"

Rob ran a gentle finger down the back of Smudge's head.

"Thanks," he whispered.

Now she had Smudge snuggled up and purring in her arms again, Olivia felt like she could forgive anything. Smudge pressed closer against her, looking nervously at Rob.

"It's OK, Smudge." She tickled him under the chin. "Rob's not going to hurt you." She smiled at Rob, only a small smile, but she got a huge one back.

Lucie reached out to rub Smudge's ears. "He's gorgeous. You're so lucky, Olivia!"

Olivia smiled. She was. Lucky to have Smudge – and even more lucky to have him back safe.

The Kitten Nobody Wanted

For everyone remembering a much-missed cat

Chapter One

"Oh, Mia, look! I told you Mrs Johnston had a new cat. Isn't she gorgeous? So fluffy!" Mia's mum stroked the little black cat, who was sitting proudly on Mrs Johnston's front wall.

Mia's best friend Emily tickled the purring cat under the chin. "She's so lovely!"

Mia's mum looked over at Mia hopefully, then sighed. She hadn't even glanced up as Mum and Emily petted the cat. She was staring firmly at her school shoes as she marched on down the road. It was as if she hadn't heard.

Mum and Emily exchanged worried looks, and hurried after her. Emily lived a few doors down from Mia, and the girls usually walked to school together. Their mums and Mia's gran took it in turns to go with them, now that Emily's big sister Leah had started secondary school. Gran lived in a little flat at the side of Mia's house, and looked after Mia when her parents were working. She'd moved in with them a few years ago, when she'd been ill and it had been difficult for her to live on her own.

"See you tomorrow, Mia!" Emily called, as she turned into her drive.

"Bye! Call me if you get stuck on that homework!" Mia was very good at maths, and Emily wasn't. Emily had been moaning about their maths homework all the way back from school.

Mia flung off her coat and hurried upstairs before Mum could start going on about Mrs Johnston's gorgeous cat again. She could hear her mum asking her if she was OK, if she wanted a drink or a chat, but she ignored her.

Mia just didn't want to hear. She'd never realized before how many cats there were in her road, or on the way to school. Now that she couldn't bear to see them, there seemed to be cats everywhere.

She slumped down on her bed, and looked sadly at the navy blue fleece blanket spread over her duvet at the end. It had a pattern of little cat faces scattered over it – and there were still ginger hairs clinging on to it here and there. Sandy had slept on it every night, for as long as Mia could remember. She still woke up in the middle of the night expecting her old cat to be there – sometimes she even reached down to stroke him, waiting for his sleepy purr as he felt her move. It was so hard to believe that he was really gone.

She looked at the photo on her windowsill. It had been taken a couple of months earlier, at the beginning of the summer holidays, just a few weeks before Sandy died. He was looking thin, and they'd taken him to the vet's, but that day he'd been enjoying the late summer sun in the garden, and Mia had been sure he was getting better. Looking back now, she realized that he hadn't been jumping and pouncing and chasing the butterflies like he usually did, just lying quietly in the sun. But she hadn't wanted to believe that there was anything wrong with him.

Tears stung her eyes as she stroked the glass over the photo, wishing she had the real Sandy snuggled up on her lap.

How could Mum keep pointing out other cats, and expecting her to want to stop and stroke them? Dad had even suggested going to the cat rescue centre to look for a kitten! Mia didn't want a kitten, ever. She was never going to replace her beautiful Sandy.

Mum was calling her from downstairs, asking if she wanted a snack. Brushing the tears away, Mia carefully straightened Sandy's blanket, and went down to the kitchen.

She could tell that Mum was watching her worriedly as she ate her apple. It only made her feel worse.

"Shall I go and fill up the bird feeder?" she asked, wanting an excuse to leave the room. Mia knew Mum was only trying to help, but she really wasn't, and any minute now she was going to start talking about kittens again, or getting a rabbit, like she'd suggested yesterday.

Mia grabbed the bag of bird food from the cupboard, and let herself out of the back door, taking a deep breath of relief. A blackbird skittered out of her way as she went over to refill the feeder, and she murmured to it soothingly as she unhooked the wire case.

"It's all right, I'll be gone in a minute. And I'll probably drop bits, you can come and peck them up." She poured in the seed, and then hung up the feeder and perched on the arm of the bench, shivering a little in the autumn sun. She didn't want to go back inside just yet.

All of a sudden, a damp nose butted her hand, and Mia jumped, a strange, silly hope flooding into her.

But when she turned round, it wasn't her beautiful Sandy playing tricks on her. It was a pretty, plump white cat, with blue eyes, and Mia recognized her. Silky, her friend Emily's cat.

"Hi, Silky," she whispered. "You look a bit round, pusscat. Emily needs to stop giving you so many treats."

Silky rubbed up against her affectionately. Cats always liked Mia, and Silky knew her anyway, as Mia spent loads of time over at Emily's house. Sandy had known Emily too, although he'd always chased Silky if she came into his garden.

This garden.

Mia swallowed and gently pushed Silky away, then walked swiftly back into the house.

Her mum was standing by the kitchen window – she'd been watching, and she sighed, very quietly, as Mia hurried back inside.

"Are you OK, sweetheart?" she asked.

"I'm going to do my homework," Mia muttered, trying not to sound tearful. She was so sick of people worrying about her. Dad had talked to her for ages at breakfast that morning about Sandy. But she was perfectly all right! Why couldn't everyone just leave her alone?

Chapter Two

Mia and her gran called for Emily on their way to school the next morning. Emily waved at them through the front window as they walked up, and then she disappeared, and flung open the door.

"Guess what!" Emily shrieked.

Mia shook her head, laughing, as Emily came running down the path.

"What? You finished the maths homework and it was easy?"

Emily shuddered and made a face. "No, it was awful, I don't even want to think about it. I'll have to tell you – you'll never guess. We think Silky might be going to have kittens!"

Gran smiled delightedly, and Mia gasped. "What, really? Kittens? When will she have them?"

"We're not quite sure. Mum's going to take her to the vet's today to check. We were looking at her last night, and we just realized how big she'd got round the middle! Mum's a bit annoyed though... Well, she's excited, but she says it's going to be a big fuss, and we'll have to find homes for all the kittens." Emily frowned. "But me and

Leah are going to work on Mum to let us keep one of them."

"Oh, wow…" Mia murmured. "You know, Silky came into our garden yesterday, and I thought she was looking a bit plump. But I didn't realize she was having kittens!" *I only looked at her for a moment before I pushed her away,* Mia added in her head, feeling a bit guilty.

Emily chattered on happily about the kittens all the way to school, wondering how many there would be, and whether they'd be white like Silky.

Mia joined in with a comment here and there, but thoughts were buzzing around inside her head. She still loved cats, of course she did. But it was definitely hard to be around them right now, when every cat seemed to remind her so much of Sandy. It wouldn't be so difficult if her mum and dad weren't so keen for them to get another pet – they seemed to think Mia needed another cat to get over Sandy properly. And now Emily was all excited about kittens as well…

"What's the matter, Mia? You've gone all quiet," Emily asked, as they waved to Gran and went in through the school gates.

Mia smiled and shook her head. "I'm fine. I'm glad I'm walking home with you and my mum today – can we pop in and see Silky, and ask your mum what the vet said?" She was trying hard to sound excited, like she knew she should, and it must have worked, because Emily beamed at her.

"Of course you can!" Emily said, giving her a hug. "I can't wait to tell everyone about Silky having kittens! I just hope it's true!"

Emily told Mia's mum the news as soon as they came out of school. She'd come straight from work to pick them up and hadn't spoken to Gran, so it was a total surprise.

"Oh, Mia, isn't that lovely? Kittens!"

"Mmm." Mia tried to sound enthusiastic. She really didn't want to spoil things for Emily. "Can we go and see Silky on the way home?" she asked. "Emily's mum took Silky to the vet, so she should know for certain by now – maybe she'll even know when the kittens might be born."

Mum nodded. "Of course!"

They hurried back to Emily's house, and Emily burst through the door, racing ahead and calling for her mum. "What did the vet say? Is she definitely having kittens? When will they come?"

"Sooner than we thought!" her mum said, laughing. "Could be only a couple of weeks, the vet said. And she felt Silky's tummy, and she thinks there are at least three kittens, possibly more."

"Three!" Emily breathed, crouching down next to Silky, who was curled up in her furry basket. "That explains why she's so fat!"

Mia sat down next to her friend, and stroked Silky gently. She was very well-named – her fur was beautifully soft and smooth. She wasn't asleep, but her pretty blue eyes were half-closed, as though she was tired. She probably was, Mia thought.

"Three kittens to find homes for," her mum sighed. She looked thoughtfully at Mia's mum. "I don't suppose..."

Mia saw her mum smile, and glance over at her, raising her eyebrows. Emily's mum glanced at her too, and nodded understandingly. Mia could tell exactly what Mum meant – *Maybe, but I'm not sure about Mia.*

She gave Silky one last gentle stroke. It was odd to think that there were tiny kittens squirming around inside her.

"Mum, I've got loads of homework," she pointed out, getting to her feet. "We'd better go." They didn't really need to leave that minute, but she didn't want her mum and Emily's exchanging any more of those secret looks.

The subject didn't go away, though. Dad was full of questions at dinner time, wanting to know when the kittens would arrive, and what Silky had looked like.

"Silky's such a sweet cat," he said, looking at Mia. "She'll have cute kittens, Mia, don't you think?"

Mia nodded. "But they won't be as gorgeous as Sandy," she said, eyeing her dad firmly. "We'll never find another cat like him."

He shook his head, with a sigh. "No, I suppose not. But different can be good too, you know, Mia."

When she went up to bed that night, Mia lay there for ages, hugging Sandy's blanket and thinking. She'd never actually had a kitten of her own. Sandy had been older than she was, he was about two when she was born. Gran had a lovely photo of him that she kept in her little living room, one that Mum and Dad had sent her when she still lived in her old house, before she came to live with them all a few years later. It was a photo of Mia as a baby, sitting up in her bouncy chair, and reaching out a fat little hand for Sandy's tail as he strolled past.

Mum had photos of Sandy as a kitten, too, in her photo album.

He'd been super cute – with round green eyes that looked too big for his little whiskery face, and apricot pink pads to his paws. They were darker by the time Mia knew him, from going outside and roughening them up. But he was still beautiful, and his eyes were like emeralds.

Mia gulped, and buried her face in the blanket. It still smelled of him. She really wanted to be excited for Emily, but even the thought of kittens made her miss Sandy so much. She wasn't sure she could bear to see them for real.

Chapter Three

"I wonder if there's any news yet!" Emily said excitedly, as they put on their coats at the end of school. "Mum's picking us up today – I can't wait to ask her. Silky's been a bit shy and weird all weekend, then she went off and snuggled herself up in the hall cupboard this morning. I'm sure that means she's 'nesting', getting ready for her kittens to come."

It was Monday, two weeks since Emily had found out Silky was having kittens, and she had been getting more and more impatient every day.

Mia smiled. Even though the thought of kittens made her miss Sandy, she could see how happy Emily was. They hurried out into the playground, looking eagerly for Emily's mum. But she wasn't there – instead, Mia's gran was waving at them from by the gate.

"Gran! What are you doing here?" Mia called in surprise.

Gran smiled. "Silky's having her kittens! Your mum didn't want to leave her on her own, Emily, so she called me. My legs aren't so bad today, so I was glad to come out for a walk."

"She's having them right now?" Emily squealed in delight, whirling her schoolbag around. "Ooooh, how many are there?"

"Four so far, apparently, and your mum thought that might be it, but she wasn't quite sure."

"Four kittens!" Emily said blissfully, and even Mia felt her stomach squirm with excitement. "Can Mia come in and see them, Mrs Lovett?" Emily asked Mia's gran.

"Better not today," Gran said thoughtfully. "They've only just been born, and Silky will be tired and very protective of her new babies, I should think. She won't want lots of visitors. You can tell Mia about them tomorrow."

Emily walked home so fast she was practically running, and she dashed in at her gate with a wave, leaving Mia and her gran to walk on to their house.

"You're looking serious, Mia," Gran commented. "Aren't you excited about the kittens?"

Mia was silent for a moment. The walk home and Emily's happy chattering about Silky's babies had brought back that strange, miserable feeling again, even worse than before. It seemed so unfair that Emily should have her beautiful Silky and four lovely little kittens, too. She wasn't jealous of Emily, exactly – just sad.

"I was," she admitted. "When you told us they were coming, I thought it was wonderful. But then Emily started talking about how sweet they'd be, and how she was looking forward to cuddling them and playing with them. And it just made me miss Sandy so much!" She leaned her face against Gran's arm. "I'm not even sure I want to go and see them," she whispered.

Gran nodded thoughtfully. "I wondered if that was it. Poor Mia." She gave her a hug as they reached their drive. "Come on, let's go and make some hot chocolate. Perhaps that will cheer you up a little."

Emily was full of news of the kittens the next day at school. Their friends Libby and Poppy rushed up to her, desperate to know what had happened. Mia did her best to join in and sound enthusiastic, but it was hard.

"There's a black one, and two tabbies, and the last one to be born was a tiny, tiny little white one, with the most enormous set of whiskers!" Emily beamed at Mia. "Do you think you can come and see them after school?"

Mia hesitated. She could – but she was worried she'd do something awful like start crying. "Um, I'm not sure," she said slowly. "Gran's picking me up, and she said something about going shopping."

"Oh." Emily looked a bit surprised, as though she'd been expecting Mia to be more excited, and Mia felt guilty.

"Did you learn those spelling words?" she asked quickly, to try and distract Emily from the kittens.

Emily pulled a face. "Well, I looked at them… But then the kittens were so lovely to watch – they're all just nosing around each other and Silky and squeaking, it's so funny. I probably haven't learned them properly." She sighed. "Can you test me?"

Mia nodded, feeling relieved. She'd got away with it for today, but she wasn't going to be able to keep on making excuses. Sooner or later, she was going to have to go and see the kittens.

By the end of the week, Mia had run out of excuses to say to Emily, and Emily was running out of patience. On Friday at lunchtime, she told Mia that her mum said she could come over at the weekend to see the kittens if she wanted.

Mia's mind went blank. What could she possibly say, except that she didn't want to? She couldn't pretend to be busy for the whole weekend.

"So will you come?" Emily asked, staring at her and frowning slightly.

Mia opened her mouth, and then closed it again helplessly.

"You don't want to, do you?" Emily said. Her voice was flat, and Mia could see that she was really hurt. It made Mia feel terrible.

"Sorry..." she whispered.

"Is it because of Sandy?" Emily said. She sounded as though she was trying to be cross, but she couldn't manage it. Emily was useless at arguing. When she and Mia had a fight it usually only lasted two minutes before Emily cried.

Mia nodded. "It's not that I don't want you to have them... I just miss Sandy, and you having all those kittens..."

"I know you miss Sandy," Emily said, her voice getting sniffly already.

"But you're supposed to be my best friend, and you ought to at least try and be happy for me! I really wanted to show them to you."

Mia nodded. She felt like she might cry now, too. "I know! I really am trying! I just can't make myself stop being sad about him. I can't be happy about the kittens. I can't do it!"

Emily stared back at her, tears welling up in her brown eyes, and then she gave a huge sniff and raced off to hide in the corner of the playground behind one of the benches.

Mia stared after her sadly. She knew she ought to go after her friend and say sorry, and promise that of course she'd go and see the kittens. But her feet just wouldn't move.

It was a very strange walk home. Mia and Emily didn't talk to each other, and Mia's gran, who'd come to fetch them, could hardly get them to talk to her either. For Mia, it was a relief when Emily ducked into her garden.

"What on earth's the matter?" Gran asked, as they took off their coats in the hallway. "Have you two had a row?"

"Sort of..." Mia admitted.

"Well, I hope you're going to make up, Mia. You both looked so miserable. Can't you talk to her about it? Why don't you give her a call?"

Mia shook her head. "It wasn't really that sort of fight. We didn't shout at each other, or anything. It's mostly my fault, and Emily won't be my friend unless I can sort it out. But I can't..." She sniffed. She'd spent the whole afternoon feeling awful, and now she was at home with only Gran to see, she felt like just letting herself cry.

Gran hugged her. "Oh, Mia. Why don't you tell me? Maybe talking to

288

someone else will help."

Mia shook her head. "I don't think it will," she whispered. But she let Gran lead her into her little sitting room, and sat down on the sofa with her.

Gran gave her a tissue. "Go on, Mia. What happened?"

"She wants me to go and see her kittens."

"And you can't?"

Mia leaned against her shoulder. "It makes me too sad," she murmured. "Mum and Dad keep talking about us getting another pet, a rabbit, or even another cat. It's like everyone's forgotten Sandy."

Gran sighed. "I don't think that's true, Mia. Your mum and dad are trying to cheer you up, that's all. We all loved Sandy, you know that. He was your special cat, though, I do understand."

"I really, really miss him…" Mia said tearfully. "Mum and Dad won't listen to me. They think I ought to have got over it by now, and I'm just being silly!"

"Oh, Mia, they really don't think that. They just want you to be happy."

"But it was August when he died, and it's only October now. I haven't stopped missing him yet." Mia sniffed. "I can't imagine not missing him! And now I can't even say anything about it to Emily, because she's so excited about her kittens. I tried to explain, but she didn't understand."

"It's such a special time for her,"

Gran said, stroking Mia's hair. "She can't help being happy about it, can she?"

"I suppose not. I just wish I could be happy with her, that's all."

"Are you sure you want to be happy?" Gran said thoughtfully, and Mia sat up and stared at her.

"Of course I am! I don't *want* to be miserable!"

"But I think you're hanging on to being sad, Mia. At least if you're miserable, someone's still missing Sandy. It's as if he's still here. Do you see what I mean?"

Mia shook her head. "It isn't like that..." But her voice trailed off. Maybe it was, a little bit.

"Look." Gran got up, and fetched a little photo album from a shelf.

"I've been making this for you, Mia, but I wasn't going to give it to you yet, in case it just made you more upset."

"Oh, Gran! All these photos of Sandy…" Mia turned the pages, laughing as Sandy turned from a little gingery fluffball into the big, handsome cat she remembered. "He was so special," she said sadly.

"Do you know what I noticed most of all about these photos?" Gran asked, smiling at a photo of Sandy last Christmas, lying in a pile of wrapping paper, a ribbon wrapped around his paws. "He was always such a happy cat."

Mia smiled. It was true.

"Except those last couple of weeks, when he was ill. He was so tired, he wasn't really himself any more. He'd purr if we stroked him, especially for you. But most of the time, he just slept."

Mia nodded. "He didn't even want to eat."

"Exactly. And this was Sandy, he loved his food!"

Mia giggled. Mum was always getting cross with Sandy – if she left anything lying around in the kitchen while she was cooking, she only had to turn her back for a second, and a sneaky ginger paw would have swiped it. He even ate mushrooms, which was very unusual for a cat.

"He wasn't happy, was he?" she murmured.

Gran shook her head. "No. And he loved you so much, Mia. He hated it when you were miserable about something, didn't he?"

"Like that time I fell over." Mia closed her eyes, remembering. She'd fallen down the stairs and banged her arm – not actually broken it, but it had still really hurt. She'd been moping around the house with it all bandaged up, until Sandy had come and sat on her while she was lying on the sofa. He sat on her chest and stared at her, dangling his big white whiskers in her face and purring like a lawnmower. It was as though he was determined that she had to cheer up. And of course it worked!

"You're right." She turned to the last picture in the album. It was her and Emily, both holding Sandy – he was big enough for two girls to hold. They were both grinning at the camera, and Sandy looked so pleased with himself.

"Emily's your best friend, Mia. You have to make an effort for friends, even if it's hard sometimes."

Mia nodded. "I know. I'll call Emily and say I'm sorry, and I'll go and see the kittens soon. Maybe on Monday. And I'll try to stop missing Sandy so much, Gran. I really will."

Chapter Four

Gran must have told Mum about the talk she'd had with Mia, because on Monday morning Mum said she'd walk Mia to school, and they'd stop and call for Emily on the way.

"Maybe you can just nip in and see the kittens," Mum suggested. "Not for long though, because you and Emily can't be late for school. OK?"

Mia nodded, and gave her mum a quick hug. She could see what Mum was doing. She was giving Mia a chance to see the kittens for just a couple of minutes. If it made her too sad, they could say they had to get to school.

Emily and her mum were waiting for them at the door. Mum had probably texted Emily's mum, Mia decided, feeling a sudden rush of love for Mum and Gran, worrying about her and trying to make everything OK again. The fussing had got on her nerves before, but they were only being nice.

"Come and see, come and see!" Emily grabbed her. "We came down this morning and they'd opened their eyes. They're so cute!" She stopped pulling Mia along and looked at her worriedly.

"You still want to see them, don't you?"

Mia nodded. "Of course. And I'm sorry I've been such a grump."

"Oh, you weren't!" Emily hugged her.

Mia was still anxious as she followed Emily into the warm kitchen. Silky and the kittens had a little sort of pen that Emily's mum had made out of bits of old bookcase. It was close to the radiator to make sure the kittens stayed warm.

"Just look at them," Emily said proudly. "Aren't they the most beautiful things you've ever seen?"

Mia glanced at the pen, and Silky yawned hugely and stared back at her. She looked as though she agreed with Emily entirely, and she expected Mia to agree too. There was a definite look of smug pride on her pretty white face as she gazed down at her new family.

The kittens were wriggling about next to their mum. Just as Mia leaned closer, the black kitten, who seemed to be the biggest, although it was hard to tell, climbed right on top of the tiny white one, who gave an indignant squeak.

"Oh no! Is he OK?" Mia asked anxiously, but Emily only giggled.

"I'm sure he is. They do that all the time! I wondered if it would get better when they opened their eyes, but they still just walk all over each other. And they're so greedy and pushy about getting to Silky for their milk."

"He's the boy, isn't he? The little white one?" Emily had told Mia that they'd worked out there were three girls and one boy.

Emily nodded. "He's cute, isn't he?"

"They all are." Mia crouched down by the pen, glancing at Silky first to check she wasn't bothered. But the white cat looked as though she was enjoying showing off her babies. The two tabby kittens were suckling, and the black one was trying to reach Silky's side too. But the little white kitten stayed curled up near his mum's front paws. He yawned, and then gazed up at Mia with dark, dark blue eyes.

Mia knew that he was so small he probably couldn't see her very well, but somehow he seemed to be looking straight at her, and he wrinkled his nose and mewed a tiny little mew. Mia smiled, and reached out her fingers for the kitten to sniff. How could she have thought anything so lovely would make her sad?

Somehow after that, Mia found that the thought of the kittens didn't upset her any more. Maybe it was because none of them was ginger, like her Sandy. They were themselves instead, and although she still missed Sandy, the kittens were so cute they mostly just made her laugh. Especially the white kitten, who seemed so loving. He always nuzzled at her and licked her fingers.

One Friday afternoon, a couple of weeks after they were born, Mia went to tea at Emily's house. She was really looking forward to it. She'd popped in to see the kittens quite a few times since her first visit, but only quickly.

Somehow there hadn't been a chance to spend proper time with the kittens.

Mia followed Emily into the kitchen. It was two or three days since she'd seen the kittens, and she gasped as she got closer to their pen.

"They're so much bigger!"

Emily laughed. "I know! It's amazing, isn't it?"

Mia shook her head. "It's like someone's blown them up, like little furry balloons..." She crouched down to look more closely at the four kittens in their pen. One of the tabbies was stomping determinedly across the soft blankets on the floor, while the other three were feeding. "They look more cat-shaped, somehow. Do you know what I mean? They were just tiny fluffy balls before, but now they're mini-cats. Oh, look…"

The white kitten seemed to have heard her talking. He stopped feeding, and looked around curiously, trying to work out where her voice was coming from. Then he stumbled towards her, uttering that tiny squeak of a mew she'd heard before.

"Hello, sweetie," Mia whispered, and the kitten mewed back, trying to scrabble his way up the side of the pen.

"Wow! He's never done that before!" Emily murmured, her eyes wide.

"Can I pick him up?" Mia asked hopefully. "Would Silky mind?"

Silky was still feeding one of the tabbies and the black kitten, but she had her head up, and she was watching Mia and the white kitten carefully.

"It should be OK, don't you think, Mum?" Emily asked. "We've picked them up before, and you can see he wants you to!"

Very gently, Mia reached into the pen and scooped up the white kitten, snuggling him carefully in her lap.

The kitten let out a little breath of a purr, padding at her school skirt with his paws. Then he curled up with a contented sigh. This was what he had wanted.

"He's so soft!" Mia whispered. "And I'm sure his whiskers have grown since I last saw him. Just look at them!"

The kitten stared up at her. He liked her voice. He recognized it from when she had come before, and the girl's smell. She had stroked him, and he'd wanted her to cuddle him. He yawned and his waterfall of white whiskers shimmered.

"None of the others have whiskers like that!" Mia laughed. "You should call him Whiskers, Emily. You haven't named them yet, have you?"

Emily shook her head. She had a huge smile suddenly. "Well, we've only named the black kitten, because we're keeping her! She's going to be my birthday present!" She picked up the black kitten, who seemed to have fallen asleep while she was feeding. "I'm calling her Satin, to go with Silky, you see?" She snuggled the kitten under her chin lovingly.

"You're so lucky!" Mia smiled, but her stomach turned over. Of course. The kittens would have to go to new owners. She sighed, and the white kitten made a little grumbling noise as his comfy lap shifted. She'd only known Whiskers – she couldn't help calling him that, even though she knew it wouldn't be his real name – for a couple of weeks, but already she knew she would miss him.

Chapter Five

Whiskers wriggled himself further into the cosy fold of the blanket. He was still only very tiny, but he was starting to understand more about the world, and today the world felt *cold*. He didn't like it. Usually he would have snuggled up next to his mother, but she had disappeared. Now that he and his sisters were a bit bigger, nearly four weeks old, she did that every so often.

Something soft landed in the pen next to him, and Whiskers twitched and woke out of his half-doze. It was a big, round, bright pink thing. He had no idea what it was. Neither did his two tabby sisters, who prowled towards it together, hissing fiercely. They were very good at being fierce. Whiskers and Satin watched worriedly as one of the tabby kittens dabbed a paw at the pink thing. It bounced a little. She tapped it again, and it wobbled in an interesting sort of way, so she jabbed at it with her claws out, this time.

The balloon burst with an enormous bang, and the tabby kittens jumped back in surprise, eyeing the shrivelled bit of pink rubber that was left. Whiskers cowered back in the corner of the pen, mewing with fright and wishing his mother would come. He had no idea what had happened! How had the round pink thing disappeared, and why had there been that terrible noise?

Silky shot back into the room, convinced that someone was hurting her babies, and leaped into the pen, checking them all frantically. Whiskers pressed up against her, shivering.

"I'm sorry, kittens." Emily crouched down by the pen. "I didn't mean to scare you. It was only a balloon – I'm blowing them up for my birthday party, and that pink one must have rolled off the table."

Whiskers mewed again, eyeing the other strange round pink things he could see on the kitchen table. Did that mean there were going to be more horrible noises? When Emily tried to give him a comforting stroke he let her, but he was trembling, and showing his tiny little teeth.

"Oh no…" Emily said sadly. "It really scared you, didn't it? Never mind, I've got some good news. Mia's coming later, and she's staying the night. That'll be nice, won't it? You love Mia, don't you?" She sighed to herself, almost crossly. "And Mia loves you too, she just doesn't know it yet."

Mia had been visiting the kittens almost every day, and she always made straight for Whiskers. "I wish she'd just hurry up and work out that she should take you home," Emily told Whiskers sadly. "Mum's already talking about looking for new homes for you in a few weeks' time. I've given Mia loads of hints, but she doesn't get them at all, and I don't want to come out and say it in case it makes her miserable about Sandy again."

She tickled Whiskers behind the ears. "You want to be Mia's kitten, don't you, Whiskers? You never play as nicely with anyone else. And you're always sad when she goes home. You mewed after her yesterday, and you looked really lonely, even though you were cuddled up next to Silky." She sighed. "Anyway, you'll all have to be super-cute tonight for my sleepover," she told the kittens, half-seriously. "Mia's coming, and Libby and Poppy. At least, they are if it doesn't snow before then. It's so cold now! You'd better groom your babies, Silky. Put their party fur on!"

"Oh, did you do all the balloons, Emily? Good. I'll hang them up in the hall, you go and get changed. Leah's just putting the birthday banner on the front door." Emily's mum hurried into the kitchen, and gave her a quick hug. "Are you excited about your party?"

Emily nodded, laughing. "Course I am. But it's so chilly! I'm not sure about sleeping on the living-room floor now!"

Her mum nodded. "I know, I hope it

doesn't get too much colder before Christmas, it's still only November."

Leah came in, rubbing her fingers. "I'm frozen," she moaned, but then her eyes widened. "Hey, look at Satin!"

The black kitten was teetering on the edge of the pen, and as they watched, she half-jumped, half-fell on to the kitchen floor, where she stood up and shook herself, trying to look as though she meant to do exactly that.

"Oh, my goodness…" Mum muttered. "We're in for it now. They'll be everywhere. We must remember to keep the kitchen door closed. They would choose today of all days!"

314

The two tabby kittens were now standing on their back legs, peering over the top of the pen and staring at their sister with huge, round eyes, as though they couldn't believe what she'd managed to do. Satin had set off to investigate the kitchen and was sniffing thoughtfully around the table legs.

"Shall I let her explore for a bit?" Emily asked, and Mum nodded.

"I expect she'll wear herself out quite soon. Go and get changed – they'll all be here in a minute! Just make sure you shut the kitchen door!"

Mia looked at the kittens a little anxiously. Libby and Poppy had just arrived, and the kitchen had suddenly got very noisy. She hoped Silky and the kittens wouldn't mind.

But Satin and the two tabby kittens were loving the attention. They put on a beautiful performance of stalking a piece of wool, and then climbed all over Libby and Poppy. Satin then snuggled up on Libby's knee, while the tabbies fought each other for the wool. Only Whiskers was still in the kitten pen, hiding behind Silky.

"The little white kitten's so cute!" Poppy said, reaching into the pen to pick him up. Whiskers shied away from her, but she didn't seem to notice – she grabbed him, and took him out of his lovely safe pen, dangling him in front of her.

"Don't scare him…" Mia said worriedly. She was itching to snatch Whiskers away from Poppy – it wasn't that Poppy meant to frighten him, she just didn't know how to hold him properly. But Whiskers wasn't hers. She couldn't boss Poppy around. And if Mia grabbed him, he'd only be even more scared. Emily was out of the room, helping her mum put everyone's coats away, or Mia knew she'd have said something.

Poppy sat down on the floor, placing Whiskers on her lap and stroking him. But he was upset now, and he hissed and dug in his claws as he scrambled to get away from the loud, scary girl.

Poppy squeaked. "Ow, he scratched me!" She jerked her leg, and Whiskers slipped off her lap, landing on the floor with a worried mew.

"Sshh, sshh… Come here, Whiskers." Mia stretched out a hand to him gently, and he gladly crept over to her, burrowing into her skirt as she put him on her lap.

"He didn't mean to scratch you," she told Poppy. "He's just a bit shyer than the other kittens."

Poppy nodded. "He's sweet, but I like the tabby ones more. They've got such

cute tricks! Oh,
look, that one's got
wool all wrapped round her paws!"

Mia stroked Whiskers and sighed.
He had cute tricks too, like the way his
huge whiskers wobbled when he
yawned, and the way he always put his
front paws in the food bowl, now that
the kittens were starting on solid food.
It was just that Satin and the tabbies
were so much bouncier, everyone
always noticed them first.

"You need to be a bit more friendly,"
she whispered to Whiskers. "You won't
find an owner if you keep hiding in your
pen. People will be coming to see if they
want to take you home, a few weeks
from now. You've got to show everybody
how gorgeous you are." She smiled,

rather sadly. She wanted Whiskers to have a lovely home of his own, but if he stayed at Emily's, it meant she'd be able to carry on seeing him. Emily's mum kept saying they were only keeping Satin, but if they couldn't find a nice owner for Whiskers, she might change her mind...

Whiskers didn't know what Mia was saying, but he liked listening to her, and she made him feel safe. He purred, very quietly, and nuzzled her hand.

"Shall we watch the film in our sleeping bags?" Emily suggested, as she took a bowl of popcorn out of the microwave. "Oh, this smells fab."

"Definitely sleeping bags," Poppy agreed.

"Can we bring the kittens?" Libby asked hopefully.

Emily's mum looked thoughtful. "I suppose for a bit. But they'll probably want to be back with Silky soon. And after the film, girls, you need to go to sleep! It's getting late."

The girls all nodded angelically, but Emily winked at Mia behind her mum's back. "I've got a secret chocolate supply," she whispered. "Are you bringing Whiskers?"

Mia nodded. "If you think he won't mind. He prefers being in his pen, doesn't he?"

Emily shook her head. "Not if it's you cuddling him."

Mia went pink. "Do you think he likes me that much?"

Emily rolled her eyes. "Of course he does! Come on!"

Mia went into the living room, and snuggled up in her sleeping bag – even with the heating on high, it was still chilly. Emily's mum had said they'd better all sleep in a huddle to keep warm, like penguins, and she'd found loads of extra blankets. Whiskers sat on Mia's tummy, purring quietly to himself. He was happy. He hadn't been sure about the loud girls, and people grabbing him, but now he had Mia, and she didn't seem to be going anywhere, like she usually was. He could even put up with the noisy girls if Mia was there too.

Mia hardly paid attention to the film at all. She was watching Whiskers, snuggled up on her sleeping bag and stroking him gently. His fur was so soft – and he was such a little cat, so different from Sandy.

As the film went on, the other kittens padded back to the kitchen, looking for Silky and their pen. But Whiskers curled up on top of Mia, and fell fast asleep – and he was still there the next morning.

Chapter Six

"Oh, Mia!" Dad laughed. "How did you get him to do that?" He'd just arrived to pick Mia up from the sleepover. Libby and Poppy had already gone; they had to hurry off to a dance class.

Mia shook her head, very, very carefully. "I didn't, Dad. He just climbed up there. I think he's eyeing my toast."

From his place on her shoulder, Whiskers purred loudly, and Mia giggled as his long whiskers tickled her cheek. "I wish I didn't have to go home and say goodbye to you!"

Her dad exchanged a thoughtful glance with Emily's mum. "When will the kittens be ready to go to new homes?"

"Well, I was looking it up, and it seems that about ten or twelve weeks old would be best. Ours are four weeks now, so they'll be ten weeks old about halfway through December. So I thought around then. It's a bit close to Christmas, that's the only problem. Everyone's so busy, and I don't want to be encouraging people to give kittens as presents."

"Why not?" Mia asked. She thought a kitten would be a lovely Christmas present. Emily was having Satin for her birthday, after all.

"Well, people sometimes get a kitten for their children at Christmas, and don't really think about them growing up into big cats who need looking after. Then sometimes they're abandoned," Emily's mum added sadly. "Luckily, most kittens get born in the spring or summertime. Silky was a bit late!"

Mia reached up and tickled Whiskers under the chin. She could feel his purrs buzzing against her neck.

I could take you home, she thought to herself, just for a second. But then she remembered. She didn't want another cat – not after Sandy. Very gently, she reached up, and lifted Whiskers off her shoulder, and took him over to the pen. "Sorry, sweetheart, I have to go."

Whiskers stared after her in surprise. Had Mia not liked him sitting on her shoulder? Why was she going? He wailed – a loud, sad kitten wail that made Mia flinch as she scuttled into the hallway to grab her stuff.

She said goodbye to Emily quickly. She felt bad, rushing off, but she just couldn't stay any longer. She was almost silent on the walk home, even though Dad kept trying to ask about the party.

"Mia, have you thought…?" Dad started, as they carried her things into the house. "Emily's mum talking about homes for the kittens made me wonder. You seem to get on so well with Whiskers…"

He trailed off when Mia looked up at him with her eyes full of tears.

"I can't," she whispered. "I thought I could, but what about Sandy? I'm not going to forget him! I never, ever want another cat again!"

"You don't have to forget him, Mia…" Dad tried to say, but Mia raced off upstairs to her room and slammed the door behind her.

Over the next few weeks, Emily kept Mia updated as they started to look for new homes for the kittens. Her mum had put an ad in the newsagent's, and the other local shops that had noticeboards. A couple of people had rung about coming to see them already.

"Someone called Maria is coming over on Saturday to see them all," she told Mia, as they ate their packed lunches. "I'm sort of half-excited, half-sad. I really want them all to have nice homes." Emily shook her head. "And at least we're keeping Satin."

Mia nodded. She wanted them to have good homes, too. Especially Whiskers. He needed a home with somebody who could love him properly, without always remembering another cat. It was no use Emily and Mum and Dad giving her all those hopeful looks. Sandy was her forever cat. She couldn't replace him, not even with Whiskers.

Emily's mum showed Maria into the kitchen, where Emily and Leah were playing with the kittens.

"Oh, aren't they sweet! How many are there?" Maria asked, laughing as one of the tabbies sniffed her boots.

"Four, but we're keeping Satin – the black kitten. There are two female tabbies, and the little white boy. Did you want just one kitten?" Emily's mum asked. "We're thinking that the tabby girls might want to stay together – they're such a team."

"I was only planning on getting one," Maria said. "I can't see a white kitten…"

"He was here a minute ago!" Leah looked around the kitchen. "Now that they can climb out of their pen they're all over the place."

"He's a little shy," Emily's mum explained. "But he's very sweet once he gets used to you. Look, there he is!" She smiled, and pointed to the pen, where a little white head was poking out under the fleecy blanket. "I'll get him out." She picked him up and tried to pass him to Maria, but Whiskers squeaked in fright and then hissed, his paws all sticking out rigidly, and his tail fluffed out to twice its usual size.

"Oh dear, don't make him if he doesn't want to," Maria said worriedly. "Poor thing, he really is nervous. There are a lot of cats round where I live, and I'm not sure this little one would cope very well if he's so shy. I'm sorry – I'm sure you'll find lovely homes for them all."

Emily's mum followed her to the door, and Emily and Leah looked down at Whiskers, who was now huddled in Leah's arms.

"Oh, Whiskers," Emily muttered. "No one's going to want you if you do that every time. It's so stupid! He wants to be Mia's kitten, I know he does."

Leah nodded. "I know. But we can't make her have him. Maybe she'll come round to the idea."

Emily sighed. "I wish she'd hurry up about it."

A couple of weeks later, Mia and her gran popped in on the way home from school, and found that only Whiskers and Satin were left.

"I'm not surprised Whiskers didn't like them. The two little boys were quite noisy," Emily's mum was saying to Gran. "They thought Whiskers was lovely, and they were all set to choose him, but it was just like with Maria. They tried to cuddle him, and he actually shot out of the kitchen door, and went and hid in the cupboard under the stairs! So they decided they'd take the tabbies instead." She laughed. "And they're going to call them Molly and Polly. I don't think they'll ever be able to remember which is which!"

"So it's only Whiskers now?" Mia asked, as Emily's mum made Gran a coffee. Mia sat stroking the little ball of white fur curled up in her lap.

Emily nodded. "At least he's still got Satin to play with. But Mum's determined we're only keeping one. We have to find Whiskers a home, and no one wants an unfriendly kitten."

"He isn't!" Mia said indignantly. "He's a sweetheart. He's just shy." *But maybe that's a good thing,* she admitted to herself. *I really don't want him to go...*

Whiskers yawned, and wriggled himself comfortable again. Mia and Emily had been rolling balls of newspaper for him and Satin to chase, and he was exhausted. The kitchen was covered in shredded paper, though. Whiskers and Satin had done a thorough job... He rolled over on to his back, all four paws in the air, showing off his fat pinkish tummy.

He was liking solid food more and more now, and after he'd had a meal, he was practically circular.

"But he's so different with you…" Emily sighed. "He doesn't mind playing with me and Leah, and he'll let us stroke him. But I don't think he's ever gone to sleep on me. And definitely not upside down! That means he really trusts you, you know."

Mia nodded. She didn't dare say anything, but she looked up at Gran. She was smiling, and nodding as if she agreed with Emily. Maybe she was being silly. Was it like Gran had said when the kittens were born, that she was still holding on to missing Sandy? Was she making herself sad on purpose? Maybe it was finally time to let Sandy go…

Chapter Seven

"I'll come and fetch you at about six then, Mia," Gran said, one day after school. Gran gave her a kiss, and Mia waved goodbye. Whiskers was already weaving himself happily around her ankles, purring. His purr had definitely got louder as he got bigger, Mia decided. He was twelve weeks old now, definitely old enough for a new home.

But no one seemed to want a rather shy, nervous little white cat. Mia didn't mind. She was looking forward to spending lots of time with Whiskers over the Christmas holidays. It had even started to snow that morning, although the flakes hadn't really settled. She was sure that Whiskers would look gorgeous if they took him out to play in the snow. He would be invisible, except for his round blue eyes!

Whiskers patted at her leg with his paw, asking to be picked up. Mia came to see him almost every day now, but he still missed her when she wasn't there. One day maybe she would take him with her?

"Hello, Mister Whiskers." Mia picked him up and cuddled him.

"What shall we do, mm?"

"Homework!" Emily said, grinning and waving the sheet Mrs Jones, their teacher, had given them for the project they had to do over the Christmas holidays. It was the last week of term and neither of the girls really felt like working, but Mrs Jones was known as the scariest teacher at their school. The project had to get planned, even if it was only a little over a week till Christmas Day. "We have to sort this project out, remember? Come on, bring Whiskers with you." She scooped up Satin, leaving Silky alone in the hallway, looking quite relieved. Whiskers and Satin were so much bigger now, and so bouncy that they wore Silky out.

"I can smell fishfingers," Mia said, a while later. "So can Whiskers and Satin, look at them!" The kittens were prowling up and down by Emily's bedroom door, their tails twitching eagerly.

"I think our plan sounds quite good," Emily said, looking down at what they'd written. "*Animals in the time of Queen Victoria*. I bet no one else will have thought of that. It's a brilliant idea, Mia."

Mia laughed. "I'll have the ideas, you do the writing. You almost finished the whole plan while I was just cuddling Whiskers. Do you think tea's ready?

340

The smell of those fishfingers is making me hungry, too."

"Must be. Let's go and see." Emily opened the door, and the kittens shot out on to the landing and eyed the stairs uncertainly. They wanted to be down there with the delicious fishy smell – but they weren't really sure about stairs yet…

Whiskers looked at Mia pleadingly, and she laughed and picked him up. She carried him down to the kitchen, while Emily followed with Satin.

Emily's mum smiled as they came in. "Look at those kittens! I've never seen them look so hungry. We'd better find the fishy-flavour kitten food."

"I think they'd rather just have the fishfingers," Emily said, going to the cupboard for the tin, and spooning out the kitten food. "Uurgh, this one smells the worst!"

But Satin and Whiskers raced for their bowls, and gulped down the food eagerly.

Emily's mum had just passed Leah, Emily and Mia their tea, when the phone rang. She went to answer it, fighting with her oven gloves. "Hello? Oh, yes… That's right. There's actually only one kitten left now."

Mia smiled, pausing with her fork halfway to her mouth. A paw was patting her knee. Whiskers must have wolfed down his kitten food already, and now he was on the hunt for something even nicer. She scooped him up on to her lap, and fed him a tiny bit of fishfinger. Emily's mum wasn't looking, she was concentrating on the phone call.

"Oh, you've been looking for a white kitten? That's wonderful. He is a little bit shy though, that's the only thing. He's very friendly once he knows you, but he may not want to be picked up."

The person on the other end of the phone didn't seem to mind this. Emily's mum was nodding and smiling.

Whiskers stared up at Mia, hoping for some more fishfinger. His whiskers shook with excitement as he reached up a little white paw to pat Mia's hand.

But she didn't give him any. She put down her fork, very slowly and quietly, and stared at him. The kitten's whiskers drooped. Mia's face had changed; she didn't look like the girl who'd been sneaking him scraps a moment before. She was pale and miserable. Whiskers mewed, his ears flattening against his head. What was wrong?

"Tomorrow evening? Yes, that would be great. See you then." Emily's mum put down the phone, smiling. "Someone wants to come and see Whiskers! Her name's Miriam, and she says she's rehomed a nervous cat before, so she doesn't mind if he's shy. And she's always wanted to have a white kitten. It's perfect!"

Emily nodded, but she was looking worriedly at Mia.

Mia gulped. It was. Whiskers was going to have a perfect home – and it wasn't with her. She'd let this happen. If only she'd been brave enough to say that she wanted him to be her kitten – that she still loved Sandy, but she'd said goodbye to him.

She stood up jerkily, huddling Whiskers against her tummy, and passed him to Emily. "I'm sorry, I'm not feeling very well. I have to go home," she said, hurrying to the front door.

"Mia, wait! I'll call your gran," Emily's mum said worriedly.

"It's OK, I'll be fine," Mia called back, tears already stinging her eyes as she wrestled with the front door catch. At last it gave, and she dashed down the path.

Mewing frantically, Whiskers made a flying leap off Emily's knee and chased after her. Where was she going? She hadn't even tickled his ears and scratched under his chin, like she usually did when she left.

He shot out of the front door, on to the path, and looked around. He'd never been out at the front of the house, only on carefully-guarded trips into the back garden. The garden was frozen over with a layer of frost, and snowflakes were flurrying down from the darkening sky. If Mia had been with him, Whiskers would have chased the strange fluffy things, but now he hardly noticed them. He had no idea where Mia had gone. He sat down on the path and wailed for her.

But Mia couldn't hear him. She was almost home now, and she could hardly see for tears, let alone hear a heartbroken kitten halfway up the road. She pressed the front door bell over and over till Gran came, looking worried.

"Oh, it's you, Mia! But I was coming to fetch you... Mia, what's wrong?"

"Whiskers," Mia sobbed. "I was too late for Whiskers. I should have said I loved him, and I didn't. How could

I be so stupid? You were right all along, Gran, and now I've lost him!"

Gran hugged her. "Oh, Mia. I'm so sorry. Has someone taken him?"

Mia nodded. "A lady's coming to see him tomorrow, and she's going to love him, I know she will."

"Tomorrow?" Gran drew her inside, and shut the door. "But Mia, why don't you go back to Emily and her mum and explain? Tell them you want him."

"But I can't!" Mia wailed. "I kept saying no, because of Sandy. They'll think I'm just going to change my mind again. And I told Dad that I never ever wanted another cat. Dad and Mum would never let me have Whiskers now." She sat down on the bottom of the stairs with her chin in her hands. "Miriam –

the lady who phoned – she knows all about nervous cats, and she really wants him. Whiskers deserves to have an owner like that." She sniffed. "I should have been braver before."

Gran sat down next to her, rather carefully. "I do see what you mean, Mia, but I think you're being too hard on yourself – and that poor little cat." She stared thoughtfully at the front door, and a small smile curved up at the corners of her mouth.

Mia didn't see it — she had her fingers pressed against her eyes now, to stop herself crying. She could see white speckles against her eyelids, and they reminded her of kitten fur.

"Are you sure?" Emily wrinkled her nose anxiously and glanced up, checking that Mrs Jones hadn't seen them talking. "Won't it just make you feel worse?"

Mia shook her head. "No. I really want to say goodbye to him. I have to. I probably will feel horrible, but it would be awful to never see him again."

"I suppose you're right." Emily sighed. "Miriam sounded really nice, from what Mum said."

"I know," Mia whispered. Then she shook her head, trying not to think about saying goodbye to Whiskers. "We're supposed to be writing about Victorian animals. Did you bring that book from the library?"

They got on with their work – Mrs Jones had said their project idea sounded excellent. But every time she stopped writing, Mia felt sad again, remembering Whiskers's soft white fur and those amazing whiskers! He was so different to Sandy, but he was special too. The way he always wanted to climb all over her, and his clever trick of perching on her shoulder.

He'll be too big to do that soon, though, she thought. She'd never see

351

what he looked like as a grown-up cat! Mia swallowed miserably.

She wasn't sure if the day raced by, or if it crawled. All their lessons seemed to last for ever, but home time came so quickly. It seemed all of a sudden she was putting on her coat and grabbing her stuff, and following Emily to meet Leah outside the gates. And the walk home seemed to vanish in seconds. Mia felt almost sick as they went into Emily's house.

She expected Whiskers to bounce up to her purring, as he usually did, but the house was very quiet – Silky and Satin were curled up together in Silky's old basket.

Mia swallowed. "Where's Whiskers?" she asked Emily's mum.

She looked around, hoping that he was hiding, and he was going to jump out and surprise her. But really, she knew that he wasn't. "He's gone, hasn't he? That lady's already come and taken him?"

Emily's mum was starting to say something, but Mia couldn't bear to listen. She was too late – even to say goodbye!

Emily rushed over and tried to give her a hug, but Mia gently pushed her away and ran off home.

Gran answered the door, looking excited, but Mia hardly saw her. She didn't even stop to listen to what Gran was trying to say. She simply raced up the stairs to the safety of her bedroom, flinging herself on to her bed and hugging Sandy's old blanket.

Now she had lost both of them.

Chapter Eight

Whiskers sniffed around the strange room worriedly. He didn't understand what was going on. He had been carried here in a box, and he hadn't liked it, his claws catching and scratching on the cardboard as he slid around, mewing and hissing. Then he'd been let out in this strange new place. He was sure he'd never been there before, but it smelled familiar somehow, and there was a bowl of his favourite food, and some water. The old lady had watched him, but she hadn't tried to pick him up. She'd just sat, very quietly, and every so often she murmured gently to him. He knew her. She came to visit with Mia sometimes – so why was she here, when Mia wasn't?

It was all very odd. He'd hoped that Mia might come and see him, after she disappeared so quickly the day before. But what if she didn't know where he was? He needed to get back home so Mia could find him.

The old lady had gone away now. She had hurried off when that doorbell rang. She'd closed the door behind her, Whiskers noticed, as he sniffed at it.

Or almost, anyway. The latch hadn't quite caught. Whiskers nosed it, and it swung open a little more. The curious kitten poked his whiskers round the door, and then his nose, and then the rest of him – and set off to search for Mia…

Whiskers pattered down the hallway, his nose twitching. He felt confused. Maybe Mia had come to find him after all. He was sure he could smell her. Or was he imagining it? He looked from side to side, wondering where to go. Food smells were coming from behind him, but from the noise it sounded like there were people upstairs. Stairs…

He trotted over, and looked up the flight of stairs. They were very steep.

Luckily, they had carpet, or he would never have been able to get his claws in to struggle up. Whiskers scrambled up on to the first step, feeling proud of himself. He licked his paw and brushed it over his ears to settle his fur before he tackled the next step. And the next…

It took him a good few minutes to heave and claw his way up to the landing, and he rolled on to the last step, panting exhaustedly. His claws ached. But he was up! And he could hear voices coming from behind a door at the top of the stairs. His ears flattened back. They were not good voices. Someone was upset. The second voice was the old lady who had been with him downstairs. She was doing that gentle, soothing talking again.

The door was open a crack, and he peered cautiously round it. The old lady was sitting on the bed, with a girl lying face down beside her, patting her hair while she cried. Whiskers sniffed again. He'd never heard Mia sound like that before, but he was sure it was Mia. Would she be glad to see him? What was the matter with her? He hesitated by the door, uncertain what to do.

Then the old lady looked up and saw him. She looked surprised for a moment, but then she smiled and held out her hand to him, rubbing her fingers together, her face hopeful.

She wanted him to come closer.

"Mia, sweetheart, listen. I've got something to tell you. I'd have told you straight away, if it hadn't taken me so long to get up those stairs."

"Sorry, Gran. I know you're not supposed to use the stairs. Oh, I should have told Emily's mum ages ago that I wanted Whiskers to be ours…" a muffled voice sobbed.

That was his name. It was Mia – it had to be. She smelled right, and she'd said his name, even if her voice sounded all strange.

Whiskers bounded across the bedroom and looked up crossly at the bed. How was he supposed to get up there? The old lady stretched her hand, and scooped him up, smiling. "Mia…"

He had been right! Whiskers stumbled along the soft duvet until he was next to Mia's tangle of fair hair, standing on a blue fleecy blanket. He nudged her with his nose, but she didn't notice, so he did it again, harder this time.

Mia raised her head. Her eyes were blurry and sore from crying, so for a moment she didn't understand.

Then Whiskers purred at her proudly. He had found her!

"Whiskers!" Mia gasped. "What are you doing here? Why aren't you at your new home! Did you run away? Emily's going to be so worried about you." She struggled to sit up, and gazed at the little white kitten sitting contentedly in the middle of her bed.

"That's what I was trying to tell you," Gran said gently. "When you came home so upset last night, I had a talk with your mum and dad, and we all agreed. Your dad had been convinced that you should have Whiskers anyway. He wanted to bring him home ages ago, but your mum was worried it would upset you again. So Dad and I went round to Emily's house, and talked to her mum, after you'd gone off to school this morning. We arranged for Whiskers to be your kitten. Well, and a little bit mine, for some company while you're at school. I know you shouldn't give animals as presents, but think of him as an early Christmas gift." Gran smiled at her, a little anxiously. "Your mum was so cross she had to be at work this afternoon. She wanted to see your face when you found out."

"But what about the lady who rang? Miriam?" Mia murmured. Her mind was whirring, trying to take all this in.

"Emily's mum called her to explain. She was very sympathetic, apparently.

She lost a cat recently too; she said she knew how hard it could be."

"So Whiskers is really ours?" Mia looked down at the kitten, who was sniffing the cat blanket interestedly, his whiskers looking remarkably white against the navy blue fleece. She reached out, and tickled him under the chin, with just one finger. She didn't dare do more. She felt like there was a dream kitten in her bedroom and if she touched him, he might disappear, like a bubble.

But he didn't. He purred loudly and gazed up at her with big blue eyes. He looked very, very pleased with himself.

"Yes, you are a clever little cat, finding your way up here," Gran said, smiling. "I thought I'd shut him in my sitting room, Mia, I didn't want him wandering all over the house, feeling lost. But he obviously found a way out. He wanted to come and find you."

Mia nodded. "He's sitting on Sandy's blanket," she whispered suddenly, a strange sharp feeling clutching at her chest.

Gran nodded. "Yes."

Mia took a deep breath. Whiskers nudged her knee with his nose and stood up, turning round a couple of times before settling himself into the perfect position, nose touching tail tip, like a little white fur cushion.

Mia let the breath out again, shakily. There were white hairs on the blanket now, mixed with the ginger ones.

Whiskers opened one eye and yawned, showing a raspberry-pink tongue. Then he snuggled down further into the blanket, and went to sleep.

Just like he belonged.

Mia yawned and rolled over, and felt Whiskers sigh in his sleep beside her. She'd had to move the fleece blanket now, to the side of her bed. Whiskers liked to sleep jammed between her and the wall, even though Mia sometimes worried that she would accidentally squash him.

She buried her head in her pillow and sighed happily. It didn't feel like time to get up yet. Then her eyes snapped open. It was Christmas Day!

"Whiskers! Look, my Christmas stocking." She sat up, and eyed the bulging red-and-white striped stocking happily. She could see a packet of her favourite toffees sticking out of it. "And cat crunchies, look! Your favourite fishy ones!"

Whiskers purred with pleasure. He didn't know why Mia wanted to wake up early, but he would do anything for fishy crunchies. He patted happily at the ribbons as Mia unwrapped her stocking presents.

"It's nearly seven o'clock," Mia said at last. "I wonder if Mum and Dad would mind being woken up yet? Or Gran?"

She climbed out of bed, and shrugged on her dressing gown, then padded out on to the landing, with

Whiskers following her. She peeped in her mum and dad's bedroom door, but they were both still fast asleep. Dad had said last night that his best Christmas present would be a lie-in, so she scooped Whiskers up before he could go and leap on to the bed. He'd only been with them a week, but already he had a thing about Dad's feet. He liked to pounce on them, and Mia thought that probably wouldn't be Dad's ideal way to wake up.

She crept down the stairs. Gran always woke up early; she said it was to do with being over seventy – she didn't need as much sleep any more.

"I can hear you, Mia! Happy Christmas!" Gran called, as Mia hesitated outside her door.

Mia slipped into Gran's little annexe. "You're up already!" she said, in surprise. Gran was sitting in her armchair, with a magazine and a cup of tea.

"Yes, and I'm glad you're here. I've got a special present for you." Gran reached over to her little table and picked up a flat, rectangular parcel, wrapped in shiny Christmas paper with a big ribbon bow. Gran liked wrapping presents.

"'For Mia, with lots of love this Christmas – and for being brave,'" Mia read from the gift tag. "I don't understand."

"Open it, Mia, you'll see." Gran nodded eagerly.

Mia put Whiskers down on the

floor, then started to undo the bow, and peel off the paper.

"Oh, Gran! It's lovely!" It was a sort of box, with a beautiful painting of a cat on the lid.

"Ah, you haven't seen inside it yet, open it up."

It wasn't actually a box, Mia realized, as she opened it. It was a hinged photo frame, made to take two photos, one beside the other.

As though it was made for two very special cats.

Mia smiled, her eyes blurring a little with tears, but only happy ones. On the left was Sandy, staring out at her, with his ears pricked up. Gran must have taken it just as he spotted a butterfly to chase, Mia thought.

Sandy loved to hunt butterflies…

And on the right was a picture of her little Whiskers, sitting on Gran's windowsill. The winter sun was shining on his gorgeous whiskers, so that they sparkled.

"Thanks, Gran, it's the loveliest present." Mia hugged her, and laughed as there was a sudden rustling sound. Whiskers had jumped on to the discarded wrapping paper, and was pouncing backwards and forwards, chasing an imaginary something. Maybe when he was bigger, Whiskers would chase butterflies too…

The
Seaside
Puppy

From best-selling author
HOLLY WEBB

The
Curious
Kitten

From best-selling author
HOLLY WEBB

HOLLY WEBB
A TREASURY
of
Animal
Stories

A collection of Holly Webb's
heart-warming short stories

Meet a lost penguin chick, a magical cat and a family of ducks in danger.

From best-selling author Holly Webb, this collection of short stories will enchant and delight animal lovers of all ages. With beautiful colour illustrations, this is a book to cherish.

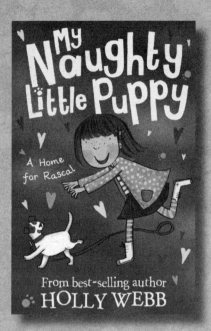

My Naughty Little Puppy

A Home for Rascal

From best-selling author
HOLLY WEBB

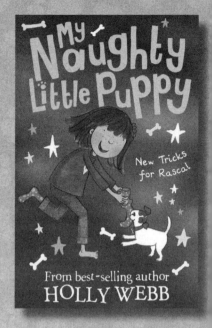

My Naughty Little Puppy

New Tricks for Rascal

From best-selling author
HOLLY WEBB

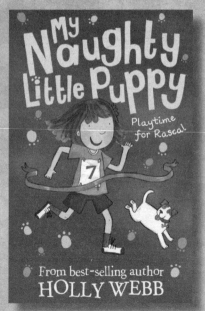

My Naughty Little Puppy

Playtime for Rascal

From best-selling author
HOLLY WEBB

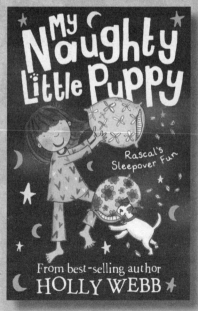

My Naughty Little Puppy

Rascal's Sleepover Fun

From best-selling author
HOLLY WEBB

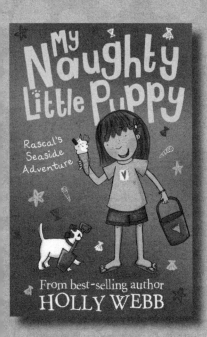

My Naughty Little Puppy

Rascal's Seaside Adventure

From best-selling author
HOLLY WEBB

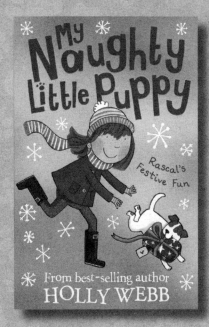

My Naughty Little Puppy

Rascal's Festive Fun

From best-selling author
HOLLY WEBB

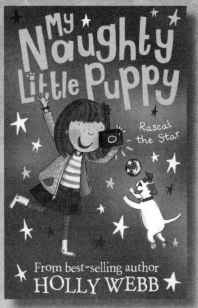

My Naughty Little Puppy

Rascal the Star

From best-selling author
HOLLY WEBB

My Naughty Little Puppy

Rascal and the Wedding

From best-selling author
HOLLY WEBB

Maisie Hitchins
The Case of the Stolen Sixpence

HOLLY WEBB

Maisie Hitchins
The Case of the Vanishing Emerald

HOLLY WEBB

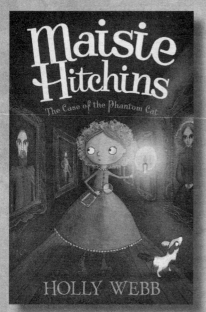

Maisie Hitchins
The Case of the Phantom Cat

HOLLY WEBB

Maisie Hitchins
The Case of the Feathered Mask

HOLLY WEBB

Maisie Hitchins
The Case of the Secret Tunnel

HOLLY WEBB

Maisie Hitchins
The Case of the Spilled Ink

HOLLY WEBB

Maisie Hitchins
The Case of the Blind Beetle

HOLLY WEBB

Maisie Hitchins
The Case of the Weeping Mermaid

HOLLY WEBB

COMING SOON:

FROM BEST-SELLING AUTHOR
HOLLY WEBB

OUT NOW:

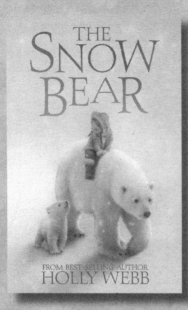

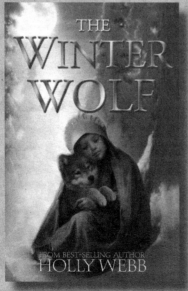

HOLLY WEBB

Holly Webb started out as a children's book editor, and wrote her first series for the publisher she worked for. She has been writing ever since, with over one hundred books to her name. Holly lives in Berkshire, with her husband and three young sons. Holly's pet cats are always nosying around when she is trying to type on her laptop.

For more information about Holly Webb visit:

www.holly-webb.com